Me, My Sister, and I

Me, My Sister, and I

Mary E. Ryan

SIMON & SCHUSTER BOOKS FOR YOUNG READERS

Published by Simon & Schuster
New York • London • Toronto • Sydney • Tokyo • Singapore

SIMON & SCHUSTER
BOOKS FOR YOUNG READERS
Simon & Schuster Building, Rockefeller Center
1230 Avenue of the Americas
New York, New York 10020

SIMON & SCHUSTER BOOKS FOR YOUNG READERS
is a trademark of Simon & Schuster.
The text for this book is set in 12-point Sabon.

Manufactured in the United States of America

10 9 8 7 6 5 4 3 2 1

Library of Congress Cataloging-in-Publication Data
Ryan, Mary E.
Me, my sister, and I / by Mary E. Ryan.   p.   cm.
Summary: Thirteen-year-old Mattie seeks independence
from her identical twin sister, Pru, by helping her mother man-
age the campaign of a candidate for city council. Sequel to
"My Sister Is Driving Me Crazy."
[1. Twins—Fiction. 2. Sisters—Fiction. 3. Individuality—
Fiction. 4. Politics. Practical—Fiction.] I. Title.
PZ7.R955Me 1992
[Fic]—dc20   92–3688   CIP
ISBN: 0–671–73851–8

In memory of Tom Kennedy,
who believed in the power of the individual
to make a difference

Me, My Sister, and I

one

~~~~~~~~~~~~~~~~~~~~~~~~~~~~~~~~~

"Styrofoam," Heather announced.

"What about it?" I said. We were sitting in the kitchen, working on our essays for world affairs.

The two of us were eighth-graders at Puget Sound Academy, where world affairs was a required subject. It was Monday afternoon, and the essays were due the next day. The assigned topic was: "What You Can Do to Make a Difference." I was having trouble coming up with an idea, but Heather, the original eco-kid, was sailing through her essay on environmental awareness.

"What about Styrofoam?" She gave me a shocked look. "It's non-biodegradable, that's what, Mattie! Don't you ever read?"

"Sure," I said. "I just finished a four-hundred-page book on Mary, Queen of Scots, remember?"

I grabbed a graham cracker and began breaking it up into little rectangles. As usual, I wondered why the graham cracker company went to the trouble of dividing their crackers into sections, when no one except me ever ate one-third of a graham cracker.

Nibbling on it, I pondered various world problems that I could solve. The rain forests were endangered, but aside from eating Peace Pops, which donated one percent to buying up land in Brazil, I figured I'd have to leave the rest to charity-minded rock stars. The economy was in trouble, but since I didn't even own a checkbook, that was pretty much beyond my powers to fix too. In fact, just about everything I could think of seemed unsolvable. At least by me.

I sighed and glanced at Heather, who was busily scribbling down ideas.

"Aerosol cans—they destroy the ozone layer," she explained. "Plastics. Fossil fuel. Fur coats. Smoking."

"That's definitely a problem," I agreed. "The media always talk about drug addicts, but they don't seem to count all those smokers puffing away."

"My father smokes behind my back." Heather sighed. "I've tried everything to get him to stop, but nothing does any good. At least now he smokes in the bathroom with the fan on."

I pictured Mr. Yamamoto, who ran a music store on Queen Anne Avenue and was normally a jolly sort, cringing behind the bathroom door while Heather patrolled the house with a smoke detector. "He must get a lot of reading done," I said.

Heather didn't laugh. She was very devout about her

eco-goals. I agreed they were certainly worthy, but sometimes, perhaps, a little sugar—brown, unrefined sugar—might help the medicine go down. Or even a sense of humor.

I was just opening my mouth to point this out when my father came in and started banging through the cupboards, looking for something decent to eat.

My father was always looking for something decent to eat. Our mother—or Sally, as she insisted people call her—was a fanatic about nutrition. She even outdid Heather in that department. Ever since Sally opened her natural food restaurant, the Golden Goat, the three major food groups featured at our house were vegetables, whole grains, and seaweed.

On the other hand, Dad's three favorite food groups were salt, sugar, and nitrates. In self-defense he stashed forbidden foods like salami and Pepperidge Farm goldfish crackers in out-of-the-way corners of the kitchen. Unfortunately, Pru and I usually found them first. Pru is my twin sister, formerly known as Prune.

"Where did those barbecue potato chips go?" Dad muttered, tossing a bag of brown rice and some freeze-dried algae down on the counter.

"Don't look at me," I told him. "I haven't seen a potato chip in *weeks*. But here, Dad, have a graham cracker." I held out the plate. "They're honey-flavored. Heather brought them."

"Bless you, Heather," my father said, biting gratefully into a graham cracker. "So, what are you kids doing inside on this beautiful afternoon?" He gazed out the window at the crisp fall sunshine.

"We're writing essays about how we can make a difference in the world's problems. Except I can't think of anything. I guess personal impact isn't one of my strong points." I stared gloomily at the blank page.

"Nonsense, Mattie!" Dad picked up another graham and waved it at me. "What about Minerva running for the city council? You could write something about that."

"Who's Minerva?" Heather asked.

"Oh, Minerva Hightower. She owns that yarn store over on University Avenue. Mom's known her for ages," I explained. "She and her women's group are working on a campaign platform to get Minerva elected."

Dad nodded. "Well, if anyone can do it, your mother can." His face lapsed into a nostalgic expression. "I was teaching History 101 back in the sixties when she and a bunch of undergrads went 'Clean for Gene.' I still remember her marching into the administration building to distribute Eugene McCarthy buttons. She was very determined. If people refused to take a button, she'd go ahead and pin one on them anyway."

"Wasn't Eugene McCarthy the guy who blacklisted people?" Heather asked. She looked confused.

"No," I said, "that was Joseph McCarthy." You don't grow up in a history-oriented, politically minded family without keeping your McCarthys straight.

"Eugene McCarthy was the anti-war guy. He ran for president in the sixties."

"Very good, Mattie," Dad said.

"But what was that 'Clean for Gene' business?" Heather asked. "Did they go around cleaning people's houses or something?"

My father smiled. "No, it was more a case of cleaning up their act. Young men cut their hair and young women wore dresses. They were trying to make the youth vote acceptable."

"Well, I guess it didn't work," I said, "because McCarthy didn't get elected, did he? And now we're back to haircuts and dresses, but the world's still a mess."

"Maybe," my father admitted, "but those kids got a lot of people thinking about things like war and peace. Besides, if it hadn't been for good old Gene, I might not have noticed your mother."

"She told me she met you standing in a line to order pizza."

"True," Dad said. "But I had to eat a lot of pizza before I managed to get in the right line. If you catch my drift."

The story of my parents' romance never ceased to amaze me. Mostly because it never seemed to stay the same. "You mean, you just hung around the student union ordering pizzas, waiting for Mom to show up in line behind you?"

"Something like that," he admitted. "But it was the

beard that really won her over." He stroked his gray-streaked beard with a flourish. "Good old Gene. I've still got that button somewhere. I should dig it out and give it to you girls. A historical relic." He smiled. "And now, speaking of history, I have to get back upstairs. The Battle of the Bulge waits for no man."

"Is your father starting an exercise program?" Heather asked, as Dad trudged out of the kitchen.

"He's working on another World War Two article," I told Heather. "He's been doing a lot more writing lately. Especially since I turned the upstairs study into my bedroom. He used to hide up there and listen to Frank Sinatra records and take naps. Now he's got no excuse."

For years Pru and I were forced to share a bedroom. Dad wouldn't budge from his study, the only extra room in the house, but he'd promised that I could have it when I sold some of my artwork. When the Pacific Science Center bought a dinosaur exhibit I made with the help of Nelson Richfield, boy genius of Puget Sound Academy, poor Dad had no choice. I moved in the day after the awards ceremony.

Although he had an office at the college, Dad worked on his articles at home. Only now he was squeezed behind a tiny desk in the back of my parents' walk-in closet. I called it the Black Hole, but Dad liked it. He said it made him feel like General Patton, laboring under hellish conditions. Personally, I found it hard to picture General Patton planning a battle with my mother's bathrobe hanging in his face, but I didn't point this out.

"Thank goodness he didn't get sick of pizza," I told Heather, as we turned back to our essays. "Otherwise Pru and I would never have been born. On the other hand," I added, "then we would never have been named after Dad's great-aunts." It still irked me that my father's relatives had to have names like Prudence and Matilda.

"I think it's very romantic," Heather said. She gazed out the window, a dreamy look in her eyes.

"You do?" I said. "How did your parents meet, Heather?"

"When my father first moved to Seattle, he had a job as a bookkeeper. He used to go over to my mom's house and do her parents' taxes," Heather said. "Anyway, my dad would hum arias from *Madame Butterfly* under his breath while he was adding up the deductions." She sounded embarrassed about it. "So one day my mom walked in the room, and he stood up and started singing to her."

"Gee, that sounds devastatingly romantic to me," I said, trying to picture chubby little Mr. Yamamoto clutching a handful of receipts while he sang his heart out.

"I guess so," Heather said. "But my mom says she only agreed to marry him if he promised never to sing outside the shower." She gave me a severe look. "Too bad she didn't make him promise to quit smoking."

"That was back in the bad old days," I said. "People smoked their brains out and thought nothing about it. Anyway," I added, "I guess she didn't hold him to it, because I've heard him sing loads of times." Granted, Heather's dad didn't have the greatest voice in the world, but then who did? Besides, if he'd had the greatest voice in the world, he wouldn't have had to do people's taxes for a living and he never would have met Heather's mother.

It was just like Dad and his pizza, I thought. Horribly, riskily romantic.

I pictured all the boys I knew. There was Cam Davis, the ninth-grade boy next door. He was disgustingly good-looking, and smart enough to be in the Latin honors class, and he seemed to like me. Or so I hoped.

Even so, it was hard to picture Cam bursting into song across the hedge. Cam was more interested in incredibly gory horror movies. I tried to remember if Cam had hummed anything the time we went to see *Revenge of the Zombies*. Maybe the theme from *The Addams Family*. But that was about it.

Then I thought about Nelson Richfield. Nelson was possibly the smartest person at Puget Sound Academy, and he had a gigantic crush on me. But Nelson was too brainy to do something passionate, like singing to a person. He reminded me of Mr. Spock on *Star Trek*. I could just picture Nelson raising one eyebrow to ask, "Why on earth should I sing to you, Darwin? It's not as if we're at a ballgame where you have to sing the national anthem. I find you highly acceptable as a companion; there's no reason I should set it to music. Besides, I have a terrible voice."

I tried to think of other boys I knew, but they seemed even less musical than Nelson and Cam. I decided my father probably had the right idea. If you just ordered enough pizzas, the right person was bound to come along eventually.

I reached for a graham cracker. As I broke it into thirds, I looked down at my blank sheet of paper. Maybe I should write about Minerva's campaign. On the other hand, what did I know about local politics? Keeping your McCarthys straight was one thing; making heads or tails of bond issues and high-rise developments was enough to give a person a migraine. I figured I'd ask my mother when she got home from her strategy meeting.

"What did Pru write her essay on?" Heather asked.

"She wrote about the Golden Goat," I said. "About how a one-hundred-percent natural food restaurant could make a difference in Seattle's dining habits." I paused. "She couldn't have spent much time on it. She's been next door practicing all afternoon."

Pru had become the latest member of the infamous Paramedics, a band headed by Cam's sister Zee. Personally, I thought her interest in music had more to do with Arthur Boyle, the lanky Paramedic drummer, than the fine art of banging a tambourine.

But at least Pru had something that set her apart—a goal, a mission. An identity. When you look alike (except for the time Pru obliterated her eyebrows), sound alike, and sometimes even dress alike, an identity counts for a lot. All I had to show for myself was the fact that I had read all four hundred pages of *Mary, Queen of Scots*. That, and the Dino-Rama. And most of the credit for that went to Nelson. He'd designed it, he'd built most of it, he'd even come up with the idea. All I provided was the artwork.

I gazed miserably out the window at the carpet of golden leaves. Deep down, I knew the answer to "What You Can Do to Make a Difference." If you were Matilda Josephine Darwin, that answer was: nothing.

I pictured Pru banging her tambourine to the sound of the Paramedics, and it suddenly reminded me of another problem I hadn't solved either. I cleared my throat and looked carefully over at Heather. She was scribbling a fat paragraph about recycling centers. Finally she looked up.

"Heather? Have you, by any chance, decided if you're going to the dance?"

"The eighth-grade Sadie Hawkins dance? Why?"

I stared down at the table. "Well . . . I've never asked

a boy to a dance before, and I just wondered if you were planning to go. And if you were, who you were going to ask."

Actually, I didn't really care who Heather asked. But I figured it was a good way to broach the topic. As a devoted follower of daytime drama, Heather could offer invaluable advice on the problem of sticky triangle situations. Namely, mine.

Nelson and Cam were my good friends. I liked them both. But I couldn't ask one without offending the other. And I wasn't terribly sure if asking two boys to the same dance fell within the rules of social etiquette.

But before Heather could answer, the kitchen door flew open. Standing on the back step, a half-eaten cheeseburger dangling from one hand, the other hand clasping Pru's, was Arthur Boyle. His straggly hair hung in his face, and his T-shirt, with the word PARA-MEDICS scribbled in Magic Marker on the front, hung in tatters. But Arthur's eyes shone with a strange gleam.

"Quick!" he said. "Turn on the TV!"

"Why?" I asked. "Did something historic just happen?" These days you could never be sure when history was going to come zooming out of nowhere and catch you by surprise.

"No," said Pru. "But we were just over at the Bun 'n' Burger, and a friend of Arthur's told us to watch *Seattle*

Rocks. He said we'd find it very enlightening. And it's on in one minute."

Pru and Arthur dashed into the living room. Heather and I followed. "Turn on Channel 28!" Arthur ordered. Pru obeyed. All four of us peered at the screen.

A smiling man with starched-looking hair was pointing at an address superimposed over his face. "Rock bands of Seattle," he said, "here's your chance to be plucked from obscurity."

"That's us," Arthur cried. "We're definitely obscure!"

"Send us your videotape," the man continued, "and you can compete in a citywide battle of the bands. Winners will be transported by chauffeured limousine to the station, where we will feature your band right here on *Seattle Rocks*, as well as arrange for a recording session with the prominent local label, Lunar Records. Next stop," the man winked, "stardom! So rush us your tape—the contest ends soon."

"All right!" Arthur yelled, raising one fist in the air. He turned to Pru. "What do you think? Interested?"

Pru let out a piercing squeal.

"I think that means she's interested," I told Heather.

"Come on," Arthur said, "let's go tell Zee. Next stop, stardom!"

A screechy rock video came on as Pru and Arthur dashed for the door. Heather reached for the remote control and began to graze among the channels.

I sighed and got to my feet. Now Pru was on the brink of stardom. A double dose of honey grahams was definitely called for. I was just heading back to the kitchen to check on the graham cracker supply when Heather let out a shriek. "Mattie! Come back here! Quick!"

"What is it?"

She was pointing at the TV. "I hate to tell you this, Mattie, but it looks like Pru isn't the only one destined for stardom."

I stared at the screen. There, smiling at the bobbing head of a *NewsCenter 4* reporter, was my mother.

"We're coming to you live from City Hall," the *NewsCenter 4* reporter was saying, "where moments ago the mayor announced that, as expected, the seat of longtime councilman Ben Edwards will be vacated."

A picture of the longtime councilman flashed in one corner of the screen. It was one of those terrible pictures where the camera catches you with your eyes half closed and your mouth half open. I felt sorry for Ben Edwards.

"Mr. Edwards has been tapped to head the National Council on Dietary Fiber," the reporter intoned. That made me feel even sorrier for him. "Several candidates have already announced their intention to run for the open position on the council. Standing with me now," the reporter said, turning to Mom, "is Sally Darwin, spokeswoman for Concerned Citizens to Elect Minerva Hightower."

"That's spokes*person*," my mother interrupted.

They say that television reveals the truth about people. If that's the case, then the truth about Sally was that she was a tiny, resolute-looking person with a knot of red hair pinned on top of her head, and that she was wearing a Save the Spotted Owl T-shirt, dangly Mexican earrings, and a determined frown on her face.

"Minerva Hightower is the obvious choice for Seattle's voters," Sally declared. "Why? Because she cares—about families, about the environment, about the quality of life here in the Northwest."

"That's fine, Mrs. Darwin," the reporter put in, "but how do you answer the charges from the Jenkins camp that Ms. Hightower doesn't have the experience to handle the job?"

Sally's face hardened with disgust. "Personally," she said, "I don't consider selling luxury cars for twenty years the kind of experience Seattle needs. Harvey Jenkins is going to find that he has one tough fight on his hands."

I'd never heard of Harvey Jenkins. Then again, my dad's vintage Mustang and the family's beat-up Volvo didn't exactly qualify as luxury cars.

"Any final thoughts on the race?" the reporter was asking Mom.

"It'll take an outstanding candidate to replace Ben

Edwards," Sally said. "But as one who understands the need for dietary fiber, I know that Ben will make a valuable contribution to the health of our nation."

"I hope she'll put in a plug for the Golden Goat," I said. "Your daily requirement of dietary fiber, available in one easy-to-find location. Something like that."

But Mom didn't get the chance. The reporter was staring meaningfully into the camera. "Thank you for your comments, Mrs. Darwin. This is Taylor Galstad, reporting live from City Hall. Now, back to you, Jim."

"Wow, I didn't know your mom was an actual spokesperson, Mattie." Heather looked impressed. Then she paused. "Exactly what does a spokesperson do? Do you think she'll be on TV a lot?"

"I guess it's a little like a campaign manager," I said. I was still in shock at seeing my own mother, beamed right into our living room in livid color. "But I wouldn't get too excited, Heather. They say everybody's famous for fifteen minutes. Only with Mom, it's probably more like two."

"But still . . . I never knew anybody who was on TV," Heather added, as a commercial came on and a smooth baritone voice filled the room.

"If you want to know the experience of true luxury, to fully savor the best that money can buy, then you deserve to drive a car from Jenkins Quality Imports."

I sat up as the silken voice continued. It was Harvey Jenkins: the man who was going to give Minerva Hightower a long, tough fight for the vacant seat on the city council.

There he was, the words HARVEY S. JENKINS, OWNER superimposed over his dark suit, as he leaned casually on the hood of a gleaming car. At the end of the commercial, he spread out his arms. "Yes, these automobiles are not for just everyone. But you've worked hard to attain your important position. Come in. Climb behind the wheel. And know that you deserve the ultimate status symbol."

I snorted. "Did you hear that? Mom's got nothing to worry about," I said confidently. "The ultimate status symbol? Who cares about expensive cars except millionaires? Regular people aren't going to vote for a phony like that!"

"Yes, but he's a phony who can pay for his own TV commercials," Heather pointed out.

I stared at Heather. Then I looked back at suave, smiling Harvey Jenkins, and I realized that Sally Darwin, Concerned Citizen, might just have her work cut out for her. Because Heather was absolutely right. Judging by those acres of gleaming fenders, it was going to take a lot more than dietary fiber to compete with the ultimate status symbol.

two

My mother looked tired when she got home. "Thank goodness the Golden Goat is closed on Mondays," she muttered as she set down a bag of groceries on the kitchen table. "If I had to throw together twenty-five seaweed salads at the restaurant tonight, I think I'd go AWOL."

Then she glanced at the counter and frowned at the boxes and bags that Dad had left behind in his desperate search for junk food. "What's all that stuff doing out? Don't tell me we have mice again!"

"Heather and I were going to bake cookies." I went over and swept the brown rice and granola back into the cupboard. Considering how often we raided Dad's potato chips, I figured it was a good idea to keep the stash a secret.

"We saw you on TV today," I added, to distract her. "As the spokesperson for Minerva Hightower. If you wouldn't mind, I'd like to ask you a few . . ."

But my mother had gone to the refrigerator and was rearranging leafy things on the bottom shelf. "Where's

Pru?" she said into the vegetable crisper. "I want to get dinner started in a couple of minutes."

"She's next door. I'll run over and get her." And I scooted out the back door before Mom could make me chop up the seaweed for salad.

The Paramedics were still practicing. Through the hedge I could hear various bangs and crashes, and then a weird, unearthly yodel as Zee Davis plunged into her featured solo. I cut across the Davises' backyard, past the deck with the hot tub, and up the steps.

Then I paused and peeked through the screen door. Chloe Davis, Cam and Zee's mother, was sitting in the middle of the kitchen table, her legs twisted into the lotus position. Her eyes were closed, and she was swaying back and forth.

I waited quietly until she had finished whatever she was doing on the table. After three months of living next door to the Davises, I had learned not to be surprised by anything.

Finally Chloe Davis opened her eyes. She smiled when she saw me. "Oh, hi," she said. "Let's see, Pru's upstairs, so you must be Mattie. Come on in," she added. "I was just trying my hand at a little astral projection."

She untwisted her legs and climbed nimbly off the table. "That's where you concentrate really hard and mentally transmit yourself out of your body into another sector of the universe. Possibly another dimension!" She beamed.

I wanted to ask what would happen if someone wanted to, say, make a sandwich while your untransmitted body was still on the kitchen table, but I kept my mouth shut. After all, the Davises were from California, where stuff like astral projection was probably a way of life.

Still, you had to hand it to Chloe. Astrally transmitted or not, she sure was a loyal mom. As I walked into the kitchen, she stared lovingly up at the ceiling. Upstairs Zee was wailing like a banshee.

"Isn't she talented?" Chloe exclaimed. "I can't wait to see their tape. Cam's going to record it with his dad's new equipment. Imagine, Mattie," Chloe said excitedly. "Our very own Paramedics—stars of *Seattle Rocks*!"

"Are they almost done practicing?" I asked. "Mom sent me over to get Pru. We're having seaweed salad for dinner."

"Oh, how yummy!" Chloe exclaimed. Chloe and Mom were partners in the Golden Goat, and Chloe always raved about Mom's way with kelp. "In that case, you'd better run upstairs and tell them to call it a night. Oh, and ask the boys if they want to stay for dinner. It's just plain old hamburgers—I got so wrapped up in my astral projection I didn't have time to plan anything fancy—but I'm sure the Paramedics won't mind. When it comes to food, they're bottomless pits."

I wanted to ask if there was room for one more bottomless pit at the table, but I just sighed hungrily and headed up the stairs to collect Pru.

When I reached Zee's room, I stuck my head around the doorframe and peered inside. The band was finishing a song called "Victim of Circumstance." There was Arthur, banging away on his drum kit. Paul, a short, chubby boy with frizzy hair, was attacking his guitar with gusto. In the corner, Clark, who reminded me of an Irish setter, hung his droopy red hair over an electric piano and banged out a few chords. I could see Pru hovering next to Arthur, energetically wiggling her tambourine.

Zee had just opened her mouth for a final yodel. " 'I'm just a victim,' " she screamed, " 'of circumstances over which I have absolutely no control!' "

I tried to tap my foot to the beat, but there wasn't any. So I stood patiently at the door until the song came to an abrupt end.

"Sorry to interrupt," I called, "but Mom says it's time for dinner, Pru. And Mrs. Davis is making hamburgers for the band," I added.

This announcement was followed by a stampede of Paramedics for the stairs. When it was over, only Pru and Zee remained.

"Well?" I said. "How'd it go? Next stop Hollywood?"

Zee nodded. She was sixteen and not much bigger around than a pencil. But instead of an eraser on her head, she had a crown of black spiky hair that stuck out at weird angles.

"It went great," she said in her customary monotone. "I think we're ready for stardom."

I watched Pru pack up her tambourine. "Speaking of stardom," I said, "Mom was on TV today. She was interviewed by a reporter on Channel 4."

At the word "TV," Zee lost her vacant expression. Her thin face grew flushed and animated. "What did she do? Win the Lottery? Get picked to be on *Jeopardy*?"

"Not exactly," I said. "She's the spokesperson for Concerned Citizens to Elect Minerva Hightower. She was announcing Minerva's candidacy for the city council."

Zee's eyes glazed over. "Oh . . . politics," she said, and clumped out of the room.

Pru rummaged around in her bag. "That's great," she said. "About Mom, I mean. Tell her I'll be there in a second. I just have to go over the song list with Arthur. We're taping tomorrow."

I sighed. "Okay," I said. "But dinner's in five minutes, whether you're there or not."

I turned and started down the hall. Then I stopped. Cam Davis stood at the head of the stairs, pointing a video camera right at my face.

"Keeping talking," he said, moving around me with the camera. "It records sound and everything."

I froze. I often did around Cam. But today was even worse. Today, when I was wearing my baggiest jeans and a stained sweatshirt, and my hair, which was just starting to grow out of a disastrous haircut, stuck up every which way, and my freckles were particularly noticeable, today, of all days, Cam decided to record me for posterity.

"I don't want to keep talking," I said, blushing. I held my hand in front of my face and began backing away from him. "Please, Cam, I look horrible."

He took his finger off the record button and lowered the camera. "I just wanted to make sure it worked," he said. "As soon as the Paramedics are ready, I'll be shooting their video. And I have to know how to use this thing. Go on, smile." He pointed the camera at me again.

I looked at Cam and smiled painfully. He should be starring in a video, I thought, not shooting one. Once again I decided that he was possibly the cutest ninth-grade boy in the Greater Puget Sound area, if not the western United States. He had curly brown hair, eyes the color of a robin's egg, and a face that belonged on the cover of his own fan magazine. I fixed a glazed grin on my face and tried not to stare at the hypnotic red light above the lens.

I was dying to ask him to the Sadie Hawkins dance. True, it was a few weeks away. But what if someone else invited Cam? There must be dozens of girls who'd want to ask him.

But what if I asked, and he said no? My tongue froze at the very thought of it.

"Er, Cam?"

He stopped shooting and grinned at me. "Yes? What is it?"

I watched the blinking red light go off, and my nerve vanished along with it. "Nothing," I muttered. "Let me know if you need any help shooting your video. Hurry up, Pru," I yelled. "Dinner's ready!"

When Pru emerged from Zee's room, I grabbed her by the hand and yanked her down the stairs. When I reached the bottom step, I glanced back.

Sure enough, Cam was taping the whole thing.

three

~~~~~~~~~~~~~~~~~~~~~~~~~~

When Pru and I reached the kitchen, Sally was rolling the portable TV into the room. I watched as she set a pad and pencil next to her salad plate. "Mattie, would you run upstairs and get your father out of the Black Hole? It's time for dinner."

"Sure," I said, as Sally leaned forward to flip on the early evening news. Some channels were still showing the late afternoon news, but in either case, there was plenty of coverage of the city council announcement.

"Mom," Pru said. "Excuse me for asking, but . . . what are you doing?"

Sally stopped scribbling. "Minerva has asked me to manage her city council race. That means I have to study the campaign from all angles to make sure that our message is coming across."

She turned back and squinted at the screen, where Taylor Galstad was once again asking her about Harvey Jenkins.

"I thought your message came across great, Mom," I

said. "But shouldn't you do some commercials or something? I mean, Harvey Jenkins has his face on TV all the time."

"Hey, I know," Pru said. "Cam could shoot some commercials with his dad's video camera. And the Paramedics could write you a campaign song." Pru pondered for a moment. "There's just one problem: Hightower doesn't really rhyme with anything. Except maybe flower-power. And that isn't really very contemporary."

"Thank you for the offer," Sally said, smiling, "but I'm afraid we don't have the budget for commercials. TV time is very, very expensive, and Harvey Jenkins has a lot more money than we do. So we'll just have to work extra hard to make sure everyone knows what Minerva stands for—increased opportunities for all our citizens, more pay for teachers, cleaning up the environment . . ."

Delicately, I cleared my throat. "No offense, Mom," I said, "but, er, what do you know about managing a campaign? I mean, don't people hire professionals to help them run for office?" I had just read an article on political consultants for my social studies class, and I was proud of myself for remembering it.

My mother put down her pencil and adjusted the sound on the TV.

"Number one," she said, "I have worked on many campaigns in my life, Mattie, so I think I know a few things about politics. Number two, Minerva is a good friend and she asked me to help her. Number three, this is going to be a community-based, grass roots campaign focusing on the issues, not expensive media blitzes. Meaning we don't have any money for paid political consultants. Or much else, for that matter."

"Oh," I said. "Thank you for clearing that up. I'll go tell Dad that dinner's ready." I made a beeline for the Black Hole.

The door to my parents' closet was open, and I could hear Dad mumbling to himself as he pounded the keys on his old black Remington. " 'The morning of the engagement dawned brightly,' " he recited in a stiff singsong, his fingers punching the keys in time to the words.

I swept a raincoat off my face. "Dinner," I announced.

"Uh," my father answered, which means, "Don't interrupt my train of thought. I'll be down in five minutes."

"Okay," I said, "but don't blame me if the onion bread's all gone by the time you get there. It smelled particularly delicious."

He sighed and stopped typing. "Oh, all right," he said. "But I really think I've got it this time." He patted the shoebox full of crumpled pages happily. "This time, Mattie, I'm going to make it. *The Journal of Military History*. I showed the editor my last draft, and he thinks if I just make a few more changes, they'll take it."

"That's great, Dad," I said. I looked at the messy box of papers. "How long have you been working on it?"

"The final draft?" He was putting the cover back on the typewriter. "Oh, about three and a half years."

"Three and a half . . . years?"

He stood up, just missing the light bulb that hung from the closet ceiling. "Research can be very time-consuming. You've got to check every fact. Military history is a demanding discipline."

I thought about all the time my father had spent lying on his sofa during the past three and a half years, listening to Frank Sinatra records.

Then again, I hadn't exactly made much progress on my own essay. "Come on, Dad," I said, patting him on the arm. "Your seaweed's getting warm."

He sighed and shut the door to the closet. "Somehow I was hoping for something more along the lines of chicken-fried steak. Deep-fried? Smothered in onions?"

"Think about the saturated fat," I said sternly. "And cholesterol. Think about smothering your arteries. Healthful eating is also a demanding discipline, Dad. Just ask Heather. Or Ben Edwards, for that matter."

He followed me down the stairs. "Who?"

"Never mind," I said. Together we entered the kitchen to ingest our daily requirement of dietary fiber.

Dad sampled the seaweed salad. "Got your campaign plans in order?" he asked Mom. "Don't forget, I've studied quite a few campaigns in my day. I'd be glad to help you in the strategy department, Sal."

"It's not strategy I'm worried about," she said. "It's the little things. Canvassing, stuffing envelopes, folding flyers, making phone calls. That kind of thing. Minerva's coming over tomorrow, and we have to make some big decisions about staffing."

"I'll help you, Mom," I said. "I could make posters and stuff."

"That's a fine idea, Mattie," Mom said. "What about you, Pru? Interested in joining the cause?"

There was silence around the table. Then Pru gulped. "I'd love to, Mom, but I can't, honest. Not this week, anyway. The Paramedics are entering this battle of the bands. It's for a local TV show called *Seattle Rocks*, and we still have a lot of practicing to do."

"Seattle rocks?" Dad looked over at Pru. "Since when are rocks more important than helping out your mother, Prune?"

"Oh, Dad!" Pru groaned. "I'm Pru, not Prune! And it's not a show about rocks, it's music. You know, they show videos and play songs, and kids from the high school dance to them. And everybody watches it, so it's very important that we win."

Dad was still frowning. I looked at Pru. She rolled her eyes desperately at me.

I pointed at the TV. "Hey, Dad, doesn't *M**A*S*H come on after the news?" Next to *Hogan's Heroes,* *M**A*S*H was my father's favorite sitcom. He could watch reruns he'd seen a million times and still crack up over Hawkeye's snappy comebacks.

Before Dad could say anything, I switched channels on the TV—just in time to see Harvey Jenkins's bland, beaming face. "Not everyone is in a position to own a luxury automobile . . ." he began.

My mother seized the remote. "Ohh, that man!" she said. She switched off the sound. "If I have to watch that smarmy commercial one more time, I—I think I'll throw this television set right out the window!"

"Now, Sal," Dad said. "Violence never solved anything. Besides, that man probably sells a ton of cars with those smarmy commercials." He reached for a slice of onion bread. "Now, if you want a bit of historical advice, you'll follow the strategy Napoleon used at the Battle of Marengo. You see—"

"John." My mother gripped her fork as if it were a dagger. "The day I decide to overrun Europe, you'll be the first to know. Until then, I have absolutely no interest in how Napoleon fought the Battle of Marengo. Mattie, turn off the TV. We are going to have a nice quiet dinner. Because it may be the last peaceful one we'll have until this campaign is over."

Once our peaceful dinner was over, I stayed in the kitchen to help Sally put the food away while Dad loaded the dishwasher. I still had to write my essay on making a difference, and Tuesday morning was looming uncomfortably close.

"Why, that's a wonderful idea," Sally said when I told her the assignment. "This campaign is a perfect example of how one person can make a difference in the whole political process."

"Could you maybe give me a few specific examples?" I said. "I mean, we already covered the meaning of democracy in last week's class."

Sally paused. "Well, there's the environment," she said. "Minerva's definitely in favor of more recycling efforts, cutting down the waste in water and electricity."

"But Heather's already doing an essay on that stuff."

Sally looked at me and sighed. "Honey, I'm trying. Why don't you just ask Minerva when she comes over tomorrow? I mean, that's a way of making a difference right there—the nuts and bolts of working on a campaign. She also serves who sits and stuffs envelopes, you know."

"That's true," I said. "Thanks, Mom."

But by the time I got up to my room, I realized that stuffing envelopes wasn't a good enough idea to carry a whole essay.

I put down my notebook and picked up my sketchpad. Winston, our black cat, strolled into the room and plopped down on the end of my bed. I took out a charcoal pencil and began to sketch. Winston was the perfect model: once his eyes closed, nothing would wake him.

"What are you doing?" Pru stood in the doorway. She glanced at the sketchpad. "Hey, not bad."

"Thanks. Actually, I was trying to write my essay for world affairs. But I haven't gotten very far."

"Oh." Pru perched on my bed. I could tell she wanted to pick my brains about something, but I decided to let her stew for a while.

It didn't last long. "Mattie?"

"Mmm?"

"Do you think we should ask anybody to that Sadie Hawkins thing?"

"What do you mean?" I hated it when Pru started sentences with the pronoun "we." It made me feel as if we were joined at the hip.

She ran a hand through her short hair, which was exactly like my short hair. Which figured, since the minute I'd gotten my hair cut, Pru had rushed out to get hers cut too. "Oh, I don't know. I just wondered if you'd heard who was going. Not that I take a dance that seriously. Because I don't."

"Well," I said slowly, trying to figure out what Pru was driving at before she got there, "it's a Sadie Hawkins dance. That means the girls are supposed to ask the boys. Why?" I added. "Did you have anyone in mind? What about Arthur?"

Pru looked shocked. "Arthur's almost fifteen! He wouldn't be caught dead at a junior high dance!"

The ultimate destination of this conversation suddenly lurched into view. "Do you mean, am I going to ask Nelson Richfield to the Sadie Hawkins dance, Pru? Is that what this is all about?"

It was true. I could always ask Nelson Richfield. Nelson would definitely accept. And it was unlikely that he would be in very great demand.

Nelson was one of those people who would probably improve with age. In the meantime, not too many girls saw his potential. I was the exception. But I still wasn't sure if unexplored potential, and excellent chess skills, were good enough reasons to ask a boy to a dance. Somehow I didn't think so.

Pru smiled sweetly. "I was just wondering. Because I happen to know a lot of ninth-grade boys are going to the dance."

"I thought you didn't know who was going," I said. "Anyway, how do you know Arthur wouldn't be caught dead at the dance? Have you even asked?"

Pru gave me another patient smile. "I just figured if no one else asked Cam Davis, it would be the neighborly thing to do. After all, he's still new to Puget Sound Academy. He's probably never even heard of Sadie Hawkins dances."

I thought of lying and saying I'd already asked Cam. I thought of disavowing all knowledge of Nelson Richfield. But the truth was, so far I hadn't had the nerve to ask anyone, and Pru knew it.

"I probably won't even go," Pru added as an afterthought. "I just figured I should ask you about it. In case I do."

"Sure," I said, as she got up off the bed. "Let me know what you decide to do."

"Oh, I will, Mattie," Pru said. She headed for the door. "And . . . thanks."

I remembered how Pru and I had competed for Cam's attention when he'd first moved in next door. It wasn't a pleasant memory. And now Pru was over at the Davises' all the time, practicing with Zee's band. I knew Cam liked me better. But Pru had one thing I didn't: all the nerve in the world.

I sighed and patted Winston, who began to snore. Then I put away my sketchpad and picked up my notebook. "Politics is an excellent way for one person to make a difference," I wrote. "Even if it's just stuffing envelopes."

four

~~~~~~~~~~~~~~~~~~~~~~~~~~~~~~~~~~~

The first person I saw when I got to school was Nelson Richfield.

"Hi," he said, falling into step beside me. The halls were lined with posters reminding eighth-graders of the upcoming dance. I prayed that Nelson wouldn't notice them.

Instead, I told him about the problem I'd had writing my essay. "I guess I'm not really sure one person *can* make a difference," I admitted. "I mean, look at my parents. They still believe in all that sixties stuff, but I don't know if it's gotten them anywhere. The world's still a mess."

"Whoa, Darwin." Nelson held up a hand. He was thin and severe-looking, with shaggy black hair that he liked to flick out of his eyes whenever he was trying to make a point. Nelson gave his head an emphatic flick. "That's entirely defeatist. What would happen if everybody felt that way? Nobody would vote, so people would stop holding elections. No more elections, no more choices. Bang—a bigger mess than ever."

"Mattie Darwin!" It was Mr. Briggs, the world affairs teacher, who also doubled as debating team coach. He paused and glanced at Nelson, and then back at me. "It *is* Mattie, isn't it?"

"Yes, Mr. Briggs," I said. I dreaded being accosted by Mr. Briggs. For one thing, my essay barely filled a page. For another, ever since the school year had begun, he had been pressuring Pru and me to join the debating team. Identical twins, he'd explained, were bound to have a devastating effect on the opposing side during a debate. "Why, they won't be able to remember which one of you spoke first, much less what your argument was," he'd said.

Now Mr. Briggs loomed over me with a big smile on his face. "I saw your mother on the news last night, Mattie. How exciting for your family! Imagine, having a front row seat on politics in the making!"

"Yes, Mr. Briggs," I said. "We're all very excited."

"You know, Mattie, I was thinking that your mother's involvement in the city council race could provide all of us with a good opportunity to observe how local politics functions." Mr. Briggs paused and beamed at me. "What about a class project, for extra credit, on the Minerva Hightower campaign? I'm sure young Richfield here would be glad to give you a hand. You two made quite a team with that dinosaur business, if I recall."

"What kind of class project?" Nelson asked.

Mr. Briggs waved a hand. "I'll leave that up to you two. You might want to keep a journal of your impressions during the campaign. Or you could tape-record a press conference. You could even conduct an interview yourself! Well?" he said. "How does the idea strike you? After all, how often do we have a student standing on the sidelines of history?"

Nelson looked at me. I looked back at Nelson. We both knew how hard it was to refuse Mr. Briggs: the man wouldn't take no for an answer.

After a moment, Nelson stuck out his hand. "We'll try, Mr. Briggs," he said.

Mr. Briggs gave Nelson's hand a powerful squeeze. Then he shook mine too. "That's fine," he said. "Just fine. But don't forget rule number one in politics."

"What's that?" I asked.

"Don't make promises you can't keep." With a warning smile, Mr. Briggs wagged his forefinger and walked off down the hall, whistling.

I looked at Nelson. "I'm sorry," I said. "I didn't know he'd drag you onto the sidelines of history too. If you're too busy, I'll understand."

Nelson smiled. "That's okay, Mattie. Anyway, I kind of like Briggs's idea. After all, you and I did make a good team. One good turn deserves another. Right?"

He had a point. "Sure, Nelson," I said. "Besides, once Mr. Briggs sees my essay, I'll probably need that extra credit."

Then I remembered another promise I'd made. "If you want, you could come over today and meet Minerva. You might have to fold some flyers and stuff. But it would be a good way to start the project."

"Sure," Nelson said. "So," he added with great nonchalance. "Is Davis going to be there folding stuff too?"

"You mean Cam?" A nervous feeling began to flicker in my stomach. Even though Nelson's gigantic crush on me had become more normal-sized lately, he still considered Cam a rival. What, I thought, do you do when you like two boys in different ways? "No, Nelson," I said, "Cam will be next door, recording an audition tape for the Paramedics."

Nelson didn't say anything, but he looked relieved. He hoisted his books and headed off to the school library where he helped Mrs. Bargreen, the librarian, shelve books.

But I was still thinking about Cam. As long as I was stuck doing this project for Mr. Briggs, maybe I could get Cam on the team, too, and away from Pru.

Unfortunately, Nelson would be there as well.

Sally was sitting at the kitchen table with Minerva when Heather and Nelson and I arrived, all set to leap into the exciting world of city politics.

"Come on in," she called. "You can help us decide on these posters. What do you think about red and yellow?"

"Eye-catching, Mom. Sort of like McDonald's." I put my books down on the table, which was cluttered with flyers and poster designs and mailing labels.

"That's precisely the point," Nelson said. "Fight fire with fire! This is the nineties, Darwin. These days politics has more in common with, well, selling hamburgers—or cars—than with world affairs class."

Minerva smiled. "You're probably right. But the black and white might be cheaper to reproduce on posters."

Sally made room for us at the table. "Minerva, you know my daughter Mattie. And these are her friends, Heather Yamamoto and Nelson Richfield."

Minerva Hightower was tall and athletic looking, with short, gray-streaked dark hair and sparkling brown eyes. She wore a navy blue running suit with a big Minerva Hightower for a Change button pinned on the front.

"Pleased to meet you," she said. As she shook hands with each of us, an unexpected dimple appeared in one of her cheeks.

Then her smile faded, and the dimple vanished. "Well." She sighed, turning back to my mother. "Have you heard the latest?"

Sally blinked. "You mean that poll on environmental awareness? I thought we did fine on that one."

Minerva shook her head. "Not the poll," she said. "It's our opponent, Harvey Jenkins. He's really pulled a good one. Remember that speech I was going to make downtown at the Women's Media Association luncheon?"

"The one at the Sheraton?" Mom said. "It's still on as far as I know. Why?"

"Because Harvey's scooped us, that's why. He's decided to hold a big noontime rally at the Westlake Center the same day. Free ice cream, free balloons—and mostly, free publicity. There goes all the press coverage we were hoping for!"

"How come?" Heather asked. "I mean, won't you have all those reporters listening to your speech?"

"Sure," Minerva said. "But guess which candidate will make the TV news? Me droning into a microphone about women's issues, or Harvey's street carnival?"

Mom sighed. "I see your point, Minnie. We'll get a paragraph or two in the newspapers, while Harvey's circus will be splashed across every TV screen in town!"

Nelson snapped his fingers. "It's just what I was saying: you've got to fight fire with fire. In other words, why not cash in on Harvey's TV event?"

Mom and Minerva glanced at each other. "What exactly did you have in mind, Nelson?" Mom asked. "We can't afford to drop skydivers into downtown Seattle, you know."

"No, although that's a fabulous idea," Nelson said. "Actually, I was thinking more in terms of infiltration."

"Like the Trojan Horse?" I asked.

"Or the Golden Goat?" Heather echoed.

"Different book, same author. Remember in *The Odyssey* how Ulysses and his men escaped from the Cyclops by hiding under a flock of sheep? Well, since old Harvey's paying for a public rally, he must be hiring people to hand out the ice cream and balloons, right?"

Minerva nodded warily.

"So, here's my idea. Hire a bunch of college kids to sign up as Harvey's helpers—but supply them with your own balloons and flyers to hand out instead. That would give old Harve something to think about."

Minerva laughed. "Yes, and it would give the city ethics committee something to think about too. Such as how big a fine to slap us with. No, it's an enterprising notion, but I don't think we should fight underhanded tactics by being unethical ourselves. Still, there's no reason we have to take this lying down."

Minerva picked up one of the banners. She tapped it thoughtfully for a moment. Then she turned to Sally.

"Let's get some of these posters printed up right away. Tell Bev to get her group of volunteers down to the Westlake Center next week and position themselves with posters and banners across the street from the carnival. Maybe we can't beat them, but we can at least grab some of their press coverage. Just make sure no one breathes a word of this to the media beforehand. If Harvey finds out what we're up to, he'll move the rally and take all the reporters with him."

Sally frowned. "What about the women's luncheon?" she said. "I thought we'd send Bev and her group to the hotel, to hand out campaign literature after the speech—"

Minerva shook her head. "Why preach to the converted?" she said. "No, I think Nelson's got the right idea. Fight fire with fire. In this case, one good rally deserves a counter-rally."

Nelson beamed. "Operation Cyclops," he said. "An idea whose time has come."

We settled down to work, folding flyers and stuffing them into envelopes. I peeled off a mailing label and was just about to slap it onto the first envelope when the kitchen door banged open and Pru came flying into the room, brandishing a videocassette.

"Want to see it?" she asked. "It's a total masterpiece!"

Ignoring Minerva and the cluttered table, Pru zoomed out to the living room. A moment later, I heard the sounds of the Paramedics tuning up.

Sally raised her eyebrows. I got the message and headed for the living room.

When I got there, Pru was crouched next to the VCR, bobbing her head in rapture. "What's the name of this song?" I asked.

" 'Terror in the Night,' " she said without looking up. "Arthur wrote it. It's one of our best."

"Oh," I said. Zee's yodels and screams certainly sounded terrifying, all right.

Pru beamed at me. "It's perfect, don't you think?"

"Fabulous," I said.

"Girls?" It was Mom. "I need you out here in the kitchen, please."

But by the time I dragged Pru out to the kitchen, Minerva was standing by the door. "I hate to run," she told Mom, "but I've got a meeting with the finance committee, and I'd better change into something a little more businesslike if we're going to talk about money. Or rather, how to raise some."

"Now, don't forget, Minnie," Mom said. "We have that fund-raiser set up next week. I've already sent the invitations out, and I know we're going to raise loads of money."

"Good!" Minerva said. "Somehow, I don't think the sign company plans to donate those banners we ordered." She looked around. "Not to mention flyers, envelopes, and mailing labels!"

Then she paused. "Oh, and Sally, I've set up a meeting with Bob Kelly, down at the First Avenue Mission. I want to focus more attention on the number of homeless people—especially the women and children—who are living in our city. See what you can do to get some reporters down there." She sighed. "If nothing else, at least we can raise public awareness and get some contributions to the food bank."

I waited until Mom left to walk Minerva to her car. Then I dragged Nelson out to the hall. "Well?" I said.

"Well, what?"

"Well, any ideas for the project?"

Nelson gave me the kind of smile a sleepy lizard lying on a warm rock would give if you woke him up. "All right, it so happens I've thought of a brilliant concept."

"You have?" I could hear Mom's steps heading back to the house. "What is it?" I asked.

Nelson pointed at the living room. "It's that."

I blinked. "A sofa? That's your brilliant idea?"

"No," he said patiently. He was aiming his finger at the VCR. "A video. A campaign documentary. We're going to advance Minerva's career with a little state of the art footage, not to mention our class project."

I stared at Nelson. "A documentary? But I don't know how to use a video camera! And even if I did, we don't have one."

Nelson sighed. "That's why we're going to enlist the help of a cameraman. I'm talking about your neighbor. Camcorder Davis."

And he pointed out the window, where Cam was standing in the driveway, aiming his videocamera right at our front window.

five

~~~~~~~~~~~~~~~~~~~~~~~~~~~~~~~~

I followed Nelson down the front steps. Cam was slowly panning across some shrubbery. He waved when he saw us, still holding his eye up to the view-finder.

"Hold it," he said. "I'm zooming."

I stood perfectly still while Cam finished zooming. Finally he put down his camera and came over to where Nelson and I were waiting. "So," he said. "What's up?"

Nelson explained his idea. "I figure the best thing Mattie and I can do for this campaign project is to make our own cinéma vérité documentary. You know, capturing people in real situations. I'll be the director, of course, but we could definitely use some help in the photography department. And that's where you come in, Davis."

Cam looked flattered. "Well, I'll have to ask my dad about the camera. He's a big Minerva supporter, though, so I don't think he'll mind if I use it. So when do we start?"

Both boys looked at me. I was digging my toe in the driveway. Somehow, I never felt relaxed when the three of us were together. I remembered my first movie date with Cam: somehow Nelson had managed to show up in the seat right behind us. It wasn't exactly one of my favorite memories. And here we were again.

Cam was looking straight at me. I stared down at the ground.

Then I felt Nelson clap his hand on my shoulder. "Don't worry," he said. "We'll think of something." He put his other hand on Cam's shoulder. "I just know the three of us are going to make a swell team."

That night, as I sat upstairs trying to do my math homework, the problems swam before my eyes. If a train left Chicago at 5:00 p.m. traveling at 80 mph . . . All I could picture was me on that train, waving good-bye to Cam Davis while he stood on the platform, sadly aiming his camcorder as the train pulled out of the station. And up ahead, Nelson sat next to the engineer, shouting "All aboard!"

It wasn't fair, I thought. I rested my cheek on the page of the workbook. I liked Nelson. He was a smart, interesting person. And Nelson liked me. What's more, he liked me for myself, not just as a girlfriend, or one half of a set of identical twins.

But the fact remained that this situation was ruining my life.

Whenever I was around Cam and Nelson, I worried about what Cam thought of me, or else I worried that Nelson felt jealous. Nelson was wrong, I decided. The three of us were not a good team. There was no getting around it: three was a crowd.

I was so absorbed in my Cam-Mattie-Nelson equation that for a moment I didn't hear the phone. Finally, on the fourth ring, I pried my cheek off the page and ran to my parents' bedroom and picked up the receiver. It was probably Heather, I thought, calling to ask if I was going to bring anything to school for recycling day.

But it wasn't Heather. "Hi," a voice said. "Can I speak to Mattie, please?"

"This is Mattie," I said. There was a strange pause, and then I realized it was Cam at the other end of the line.

"How are you?" I asked stiffly, remembering that I'd only seen him a few hours before.

"Fine, thank you," Cam said, just as politely. "Listen," he continued, "I thought that maybe on Friday we could go see *Creatures from the Planet of Blood*. I was going to ask you this afternoon, but you seemed kind of caught up in Nelson's project and everything."

I waited a full second. Then I said, "I guess it's been a little busy around here. But, sure, I'd love to go see *Creatures from the Planet of Blood*."

"Good," Cam said. "I'll pick you up right after the

Paramedics finish practicing. We've got to do one more take of 'Terror in the Night' before we send it into the contest."

"Oh. Well . . . thank you for calling."

"Sure, Mattie," Cam said. "See you at school."

The minute he hung up, I dialed Heather's number. "Hi," I said when she answered, "it's me. In case you're wondering, I'm bringing eight aluminum natural soda cans for recycling day. Plus, Cam Davis just called me."

"Called?" Heather squealed. "Like, on the phone?"

"Yes," I said happily. I could always count on Heather to grasp the true significance of things. "He asked me to see some awful-sounding horror movie with him."

"That's great, Mattie," Heather said sincerely.

"Anyway, I thought maybe Saturday you could come over and help me work on some ideas for my world affairs project. Nelson wants to do a documentary, but I'm not sure that's such a great idea."

Heather "hmm" 'd sympathetically.

"And maybe you could stay over for dinner. Mom's going over to work the phone bank, so we'll have to take care of the food ourselves."

"Sure," Heather said, "that sounds great. So," she went on, "who's doing all the cooking and housework while your mom's handling the campaign?"

"Oh, Dad and Pru and I can take care of things," I said. "Mom left us a bunch of lists and frozen dinners.

Anyway, it's only for a little while. I mean, how hard can it be?"

The next morning when Pru and I came downstairs, my father was standing at the stove, a dish towel tucked in his belt.

"This morning," he announced, "you kids are in for a real treat. Your mother had an early appointment with the Board of Elections, so the old man is going to fix breakfast!" He flourished the tail of his dish towel.

Pru and I glanced at each other.

"You know," he remarked, as he puttered around the kitchen, "I used to be quite a cook in my bachelor days."

He cracked three eggs in a bowl, then paused to fish out some eggshell.

"What are you making, Dad?" Pru asked.

"A wonderful dish called Omelette Tijuana. It's eggs and peppers and hot sauce. I practically lived on the stuff back in grad school. You girls are going to love this!"

I puckered my lips. "Hot sauce? At seven o'clock in the morning? On a school day?"

Dad ignored me. "Let's see if I can remember this," he said. "I know there was garlic involved. And olive oil. And . . . chili powder!" He began rummaging happily in the cupboard. "The other guys at the rooming house used to rave about my omelettes," he announced over his shoulder.

He began beating more eggs. "Okay!" he said, rubbing his hands. "Now, we fry up this garlic in the oil until it's good and brown. Then . . ." He frowned. "Knew I forgot something. The peppers!"

"We're all out of green peppers," I said. "Mom used them in the salad last night."

"She did?" He looked distraught for a moment. Then he turned and began pawing through the cupboard again. "Aha!" he cried. "Saved!"

He held up a small can with a blue label. "I knew these would come in handy someday. Well, girls, today's the day."

"What are those, Dad?" I was starting to feel nervous. Every time my father went shopping, he brought home mysterious things in dusty foreign-looking cans. He couldn't resist them. They always turned out to be obscure pickled vegetables or spiced Filipino relish. I used to wonder why anyone would ever buy things like that, but then Heather told me that whenever her father went grocery shopping, he did the same thing.

"These are peppers, Mattie. Jalapeños, to be precise. They give the Omelette Tijuana an authentic Mexican flavor."

"Why don't you just make some eggs," Pru suggested, "and then we can decide whether or not they need authentic Mexican flavor?"

Dad began to whistle "La Cucaracha" while he opened the can of jalapeño peppers. "Da-da-da-da-da-da-dee," he sang under his breath, as a little column of

49

smoke began to rise from the pan of olive oil. "First the garlic." He threw a clove of garlic into the pan. "Next, the peppers." One by one, the jalapeños joined the garlic. "And now—*los huevos*!" With a flourish, Dad emptied the bowl of eggs into the pan.

"Don't forget the chili powder," I said above the hiss and spatter of the cooking eggs.

"Good thinking, Mattie." Dad dumped some chili powder over the mixture. "A little seasoning"—he sprinkled salt and pepper into the pan—"*et, voilà*!"

We watched as he scraped three huge heaps of eggs onto our plates. Dad gazed at them with satisfaction. "Just between us," he said, "your mother could stand to branch out a bit, recipe-wise. Maybe when the election's over, I'll teach her a few new tricks around the kitchen. Encourage her to be a little more adventurous."

Pru and I looked at the mountain of eggs and jalapeño peppers. "This sure looks adventurous, Dad," I said. "I can't wait to taste it."

Pru poked at her mound with trepidation.

Dad smiled. "Dig right in," he said jovially. "But first, the *pièce de résistance*." He flung open the refrigerator and grabbed a bottle of Tabasco sauce. "A sprinkle or two should really bring out the flavor."

I hesitated. "Don't you think it's hot enough? I mean, it already has a ton of chili powder in it."

He shrugged. "As Julia Child always says, 'season to

taste.'" Draping the dish towel over his lap, Dad sat down at the table and prepared to dig in.

I tried a bite of egg. It mostly tasted hot. Gingerly I tried a little more.

"Well?" Dad was smiling at me, expectantly.

"Not bad," I gasped. "It's a little spicy, though."

He nodded and spread a red river of Tabasco over his eggs. Then he loaded up his fork with a heap of food. Pru did the same.

The next minute she was screaming in pain. "Aaagghh! Ohhhh!"

"Prune! What is it?" Dad put down his fork and watched her stagger over to the sink, where she began splashing water into her mouth. My fork was still poised over the jalapeño eggs.

"Did you bite your tongue?" he asked sympathetically. "I've done that before. It can be very painful."

"I don't think we're ready for such adventurous breakfasts, Dad," I said, as Pru gulped down a cup of water.

My father blinked. "I guess it could have used a touch less chili powder," he conceded. "But I'll make it up to you girls. Tomorrow we'll have something I know you'll enjoy—kippered herring!"

I stared at Dad. Things were getting critical. I wasn't sure about the guys who'd lived at Dad's rooming house, but as far as I was concerned, kippered herring would never replace Frosted Flakes.

I looked at Pru, who was starting on her third cup of water. Maybe, I thought, we could invite Harvey Jenkins over for breakfast. Then there wouldn't even be an election.

On second thought, old Harvey would probably rave about Dad's Omelette Tijuana. "What a fine collection of dusty little cans with foreign-looking labels!" he might tell Dad. "Wherever did you find them, old boy?"

And my father would shrug modestly. "Oh, they were hidden away on a back shelf in the condiment department at Thriftway," he would say, and then he and Harv would compare notes about the best places to buy pickled lichee nuts and Indonesian pimientos. And kippered herring.

On our way upstairs, Pru nudged me. Her face was still very red and her eyes looked watery. "You know Mom's kelp muffins?" she said, dabbing at her eyes.

I shuddered. "Those mossy green things? Why?"

Pru sighed. "Believe it or not, I think I'm starting to miss them."

six

~~~~~~~~~~~~~~~~~~~~~~~~~~~~~~~~~~~~

"And I submit to you, ladies and gentlemen, that Ms. Hightower's plan to expand arts education in the public schools is not only gratuitous, it is fiscally unsound."

"What does gratuitous mean?" I asked Nelson. It was Friday afternoon and we were hunched on the Richfields' living room rug, watching Harvey Jenkins taking part in a panel discussion which was being broadcast on the public access channel.

Nelson reached over and grabbed a handful of corn chips. "Gratuitous?" He munched thoughtfully. "Well, sometimes it means 'free.' But it can also mean 'uncalled for.' I guess that's how Harvey means it."

Harvey was winding up his pitch. "As a business-man, I fully understand the importance of holding down costs. Irresponsible spending is not the answer."

He laughed and shook his head. "But spending money, my friends, appears to be the only thing Ms. Hightower understands." He held up a piece of paper.

"I have here the budget she proposes for this program. And just where do you suppose the money is going to come from? From property taxes, my friends! A further burden that the homeowners of this city are not willing to foot!"

I looked at Nelson. "Where did he get that?"

Nelson shrugged. "It's probably the menu from a Chinese restaurant. He's not exactly holding it up to the camera."

"But what about art classes?" I said. "Aren't they important?"

A woman on the panel raised her hand. "Don't our children deserve a well-rounded education, Mr. Jenkins? In the last five years, these programs have been cut back drastically. Music, art, drama—isn't there a place for them in the schools?"

Harvey gave her his dazzling smile. "If the parents of Seattle can afford to pay the ridiculous property taxes Ms. Hightower proposes, madam," he said, "they can afford to give little Johnny the music lessons he deserves."

"Oh, right," Nelson said. He pushed the corn chips away disgustedly. "And what if they can't?"

Listening to the panel discussion, I felt confused. Budgets, property taxes, holding down costs . . . I still wasn't exactly sure what some of those words meant. But wrapped in Harvey Jenkins's silken tones, they sounded downright sinister.

"As you may or may not know, Ms. Hightower is involved with a number of . . ." Harvey paused. "Well, the polite term is activist groups. Personally, I prefer the word 'radical.' Between saving dolphins and owls, she's ready to put our fishing and timber industries completely out of business! Is this the kind of person we want in city government? Backing groups that will cost our hard-pressed citizens even more jobs?"

That was when I heard it. The noise from outer space. It sounded like an amplified parrot making its way through the neighborhood. As I listened to the garbled, squawking voice, it slowly grew louder.

"I'll be right back," I told Nelson, and ran outside. A big blue truck was making its way down the street. Every once in a while, a woman with a loudspeaker stood up in the back of the truck and shouted, "Jenkins for city council! Honesty in government! Let's make Seattle great again!"

The woman had bright orange curls piled on top of her head. She was wearing a red polka-dot dress with a hair ribbon to match. I wondered if she was Harvey's wife or just someone with a loud voice Harvey had hired to ride around in the truck.

When the truck reached Nelson's house, I ran down the steps and yelled, "Hightower for city council! We want clean air, not gas guzzlers!"

The polka-dot woman lowered her loudspeaker and glared at me. I thought she was going to say something, but then the truck speeded up and lurched around the corner. A minute later I heard the loudspeaker blare. "Jenkins for city council! Let's make Seattle great again!" I turned and marched back inside.

"We've got to do something," I told Nelson, who was calmly watching Harvey make his closing statement. "Harvey's pouring a fortune into his campaign, and he's even being invited on shows like this. How come they didn't ask Minerva?"

"Harvey probably donated the cameras," Nelson said. He was scrutinizing the opposition. "You've got to hand it to him, Darwin. The man is slick. A lot of people are going to be scared to vote for Minerva, for fear it will cost them money."

My head was starting to hurt. "But schools do cost money. Isn't that what city governments are for? To find the money to pay for stuff? Stuff like music classes and . . . and sewers and buses? Isn't that why people pay taxes?"

Nelson grinned and shook his head. "Sure, everybody knows that, but Harvey's got his finger on what most people really want. Something for nothing. Or rather, nothing for nothing. Just so long as it doesn't cost them anything."

"But that's totally selfish!"

Nelson got to his feet and ambled out to the kitchen in search of more nutrition. "That's politics."

I stared at the TV. Harvey was smoothing his tie, getting up, shaking hands with the other people on the panel. I watched the woman who had asked the question about education smiling and chatting with Harvey, and I wondered why she didn't kick him in the shins instead.

But she didn't. None of them did. Harvey stood there, with his distinguished silver hair and his pinstriped suit, charming the pants off everyone, and nobody said a word.

It gave me the creeps.

I was still thinking about Harvey after the bus had let me off on the corner of McAllister Street. It was something that had always bothered me about politics, and about grown-ups in general—if a person was good-looking, or had a lot of money, or wore nice clothes, people tended to believe that person. To trust him. When maybe they ought to look beneath the fancy dental work and expensive tailoring and decide what that person really stood for.

I tried to remember if I'd ever been guilty of falling into that trap. There was Nelson, of course. The first time I met him, I had definitely put him in the geek category. Of course, when it came to appearance, Nelson's corny plaid shirts and shaggy hair didn't exactly make him heart throb material. But deep-down, Nelson was loyal, brainy, and honest.

Of course, Cam was pretty loyal and brainy and

honest too, without the social liabilities. It didn't make my choice any easier.

" 'Terror! Terror—in the night!' " The lyrics shrieked out at me as I passed the Davises'. I decided to stop in and see how the taping session was going.

Cam's father met me at the door. He designed computer software for a living, which seemed to put him in a perpetually good mood. He greeted me with his usual sunny smile.

"Prune! How are you? Seems as though the session has already started, but there's always room for one more."

I smiled back at Mr. Davis, decided I didn't have the energy to settle the eternal Prune vs. Mattie question, and trooped up the stairs.

The final chorus of "Terror in the Night" was just screaming to a close on the tape. Cam sat in the corner, surrounded by a bank of video equipment. Clark and Paul were hunched over their instruments. Zee and Arthur were consulting about some lyrics. I waved at Pru.

"Hi," she called. "Want to see the playback? I think this is going to be the final version of 'Terror.' It's a masterpiece!"

"Sure," I said. "It couldn't be any more terrifying than what I just saw."

"Oh, did you catch *Creatures from the Planet of Blood*?" Arthur piped up. "Total gross-out," he explained.

"No, this was even grosser," I said. "Nelson and I were watching Harvey Jenkins on TV. He said Minerva's program would cost taxpayers their hard-earned money, and that the schools didn't really need art or music classes. Can you believe that?"

"Harvey Jenkins?" Arthur peered at me. "That import car dude? The one who's running for the school board or something? Listen, my dad bought his Beemer there. He says Harvey's got the right idea. The city forces people to spend too much money on the wrong stuff. Boy, you should hear my old man complain about his property taxes! He'd vote for anyone who promised to save him money."

I was glaring so hard I expected to see scorch marks pop out on Arthur's forehead. "Maybe," I said, trying to keep my voice steady, "your father could save money by not spending a fortune on imported cars."

"Hey, wait a minute!" Arthur yelped. "He needs that car. My father's in real estate, and believe me, your image counts for everything in that business."

"Then I'm not surprised he's worried about property taxes," I said.

"Hey, come on, you guys," Pru broke in. "Let's not talk about boring old politics."

"But, Pru," I said, "it's not just politics. This election affects all kinds of stuff—what we get taught in school, and what kind of teachers we have, and what happens to the environment and . . . and all kinds of stuff!"

I couldn't believe Arthur would come right out and

defend Harvey Jenkins, without having heard a word he'd said.

Arthur must have thought the same thing, because he sheepishly brushed the hair out of his eyes and mumbled, "Hey, listen, I'm just repeating what my old man said. It's not like I can vote or anything."

"That's true," I told him. "But in a few years you'll be able to. And it wouldn't kill you to activate a few brain cells before then. You can't just blindly accept everything people tell you. Even when it's your own father."

The moment I said it I knew I'd gone too far. Arthur shot me a disgusted glance and snatched up his drumsticks. "Come on," he said to Pru. "I don't have to sit here and get lectured at. We can watch the playback later."

"Arthur, I'm sorry," I said quickly. "I didn't mean that the way it sounded. It's just that—"

"Forget it," Arthur said. He turned and stalked out of the room.

The other Paramedics were staring at me curiously. But Pru looked mortified. "Good grief, Mattie," she said. "You're starting to sound just like Mom!"

And with that, she ran down the stairs after Arthur.

seven

~~~~~~

Sally put her briefcase down on the kitchen table and sniffed. "That's odd," she said. "It smells like burned peppers in here."

"Adventurous breakfasts," I explained. "Dad promised to let you in on a few secrets. He's going to show you how to improve your cooking."

She looked surprised. "Really, Mattie? And here I thought your dad's idea of haute cuisine was to dump Tabasco sauce on everything."

"It is," I said.

Sally smiled. "You know, when we were first dating, he used to cook these unbelievable omelettes for me. They practically scorched a hole in my tongue. But somehow I loved every bite."

She began unpacking her briefcase. I thought of telling her that even though I knew Dad was doing his best, it was hard to love every bite. Or even swallow one.

"Well, adventurous or not, dinner's in ten minutes,

Mattie. You can help by starting the salad. But first I have to get to the phone and do a little damage control. That 'fiscally irresponsible' business Harvey's spreading around is going to hurt us a lot, unless we can set the record straight."

I leafed through some flyers that were lying on the table. There was a big picture of a smiling Minerva on the front, surrounded by her grown-up son and daughter and their children. I turned over the flyer and read about Minerva's degrees in sociology, the community causes she'd worked for, and her husband, Frank, who was an engineer at Boeing.

My mother was scribbling down a list of people to call. "Is this what it was like being an activist, Mom?" I asked. "Back in the sixties?"

"Let's just say it was a younger bunch back then. My mother went to a PTA meeting now and then, but I don't think you could call her an activist. It wasn't until the Vietnam War came along and Mike almost got drafted that she started to believe that one person could make a difference."

My uncle Mike was a high school teacher. He had a gray mustache and a little pot belly that poked out of his tweed jacket. He lived with his family in Boston and was an avid bird watcher. The last time he'd visited Seattle, he showed me a rare kind of finch perched in our apple tree. It was hard to picture him as a young man. It was even harder to picture him as a soldier.

Mom leaned forward and tapped her pencil thoughtfully. "Back then there was a lottery system, and all the boys who registered for the draft were given a number. Mike missed getting called up by just a few digits."

She sighed. "It was a very scary time for our family. And lots of other families too. Anyway, your grandma decided she had to do something, and she started going to meetings and giving talks. She even went on an anti-war march with me and a bunch of students. I was very proud of her."

"But did it do any good?" I asked. "I mean, everybody talks about how great the sixties were, but . . . well, there's still wars all over the place, and terrorists, and people getting killed and everything. So what was the point?"

Mom pointed to the flyer. "This is," she said. "People getting together for what they believe is right. That you don't have to stand by and let other people make decisions you don't agree with. That's what the sixties were about, Mattie. They taught plain old average Americans the power of the individual."

"But Harvey says that Minerva is a radical. That isn't true, is it, Mom?"

"Honey, he just said that to scare people. Of course, to someone like Harvey Jenkins, anyone who thinks differently from him and his friends is automatically a radical. But he also knows that people react fearfully to words like that. That's why he says them."

"But that isn't fair!" I burst out.

Mom sighed. "Mattie, nowadays all's fair in love, war—and elections. All we can do is try to stick to the truth and hope that the voters will see through Harvey's tactics."

She patted me on the arm, gathered up her briefcase, and started for the stairs.

But there was one last thing I had to clear up. "Mom? Back in the sixties . . . did people really say things like . . . 'groovy?'"

Mom nodded. "Absolutely. Things back then were definitely groovy. And fab. And even far out." She grinned. "And yes, Mattie, we actually wore bell-bottoms and love beads and granny gowns. I remember I had this great jacket—it was purple leather with four-inch fringe hanging off the sleeves. I just adored that jacket. I wonder what ever happened to it."

"Mom," I said, "no offense, but I think it's just as well it's gone."

She laughed. "You're right, Mattie. We can't live in the past. It's time to move on. And the way to do that is to get people using their brains for a change."

I thought of Arthur's father. "But what if people don't want change? What if they believe what Harvey's saying—that Minerva's programs cost too much? That she's a dangerous radical?"

Mom looked grim. "They're being awfully shortsighted, Mattie. Taking care of the environment, educating people—those things are investments in the future. Without them, we'll all end up paying a lot more in the long run, believe me."

I wished I'd said something like that to Arthur Boyle, instead of just getting angry. Next time, maybe I'd stop and think before I opened my big mouth. Insulting people wasn't a very good way of changing their minds.

I helped Mom make the salad. Then I went up to my room to pick out something to wear to the movies. I looked at my closet and wondered for the hundredth time how my mother, who must have cared about looking cool back when she was wearing purple fringe, could have such terrible taste when it came to buying clothes for her own children.

I took down a pair of jeans she had bought at a sale. "But Mom," I told her. "These are the wrong kind!"

"I thought you kids liked jeans," she'd answered, and I could hear the exasperation in her voice. "Jeans are jeans. Aren't they?"

I gazed at the jeans, which were the wrong color and had too many pockets, and put them back on the closet shelf. And I pictured all the ugly bell-bottoms my grandmother had probably bought for Mom with the words, "Bell-bottoms are bell-bottoms, aren't they?"

I was just figuring there must be some way to teach

parents these things when Pru walked in and flopped down on the bed. "Arthur's very upset about what you said," she announced.

"I'm really sorry about that," I said. "Honest, Pru, I am. I didn't mean to upset Arthur. But you have to admit that he's not very enlightened when it comes to politics."

"Everybody's entitled to an opinion." Pru watched me stand in front of the mirror and comb my hair. "You can't go around forcing people to agree with you, Mattie."

"I know," I said.

"And you're not doing Minerva any favors, bad-mouthing Harvey Jenkins."

"Like I told Arthur, you can't accept everything at face value. You have to get the facts!" I said.

"Maybe," Pru said. "But frankly, I think you're getting carried away with all this political stuff. Barging into our taping session, blasting poor Arthur—it's positively embarrassing." Pru narrowed her eyes. "What's got into you? You used to make fun of Mom for acting like that. Now you're doing the same thing!"

I didn't say anything. Pru got up from the bed and came over to the mirror. "And you make fun of the Paramedics too. I know you do, Mattie, so don't try to pretend you don't. In fact, I think you're jealous. That's it, isn't it?" Pru's face was getting red. "Just because I have something that matters to me. Like the band. And entering this contest. I mean, I'm sorry if you feel left out, but you don't have to take it out on Arthur."

Then Pru's mouth clamped shut, and she rushed out of the room. I waited a moment. Then I put down the comb I'd been clutching and followed Pru down the hall to her room.

She was sitting at the desk we used to share, pretending to look at her history book.

"You're right," I said. "I won't take anything out on Arthur ever again. And okay, maybe I did feel kind of left out."

Pru peered at me suspiciously.

"I guess it just seems weird that we're not doing everything together anymore. But we're different people, Pru. We look the same, but we like to do different stuff. So maybe we should stop fighting it and just accept it."

Pru's eyes widened. "You mean, you actually like politics?" she said, her voice squeaking in disbelief.

"Yeah," I found myself saying. "I actually think I do." Then I glanced at the clock. "Oh, no! Is it really almost seven?"

"Why? Are you going somewhere?"

I paused. "Cam asked me to go see *Creatures from the Planet of Blood*. You know Cam—if it's got 'blood' in the title, he'll rush out and see it."

Pru nodded. She seemed to be thinking something over.

I braced myself, hoping she wouldn't bring up the

Sadie Hawkins dance again. Sometimes Pru could drive me crazy without even trying.

She squinted her eyes and studied me for a moment. "You know, that blue sweater I got at Wyndham's would look good with your paisley scarf. But if you spill anything on it, I'll kill you."

And before I could say anything, Pru had scrambled off the bed to dig out her new blue sweater.

Arthur got one thing right: *Creatures from the Planet of Blood* was pretty gross. After the creatures had decapitated their first few victims, I kind of lost interest in the plot. But Cam seemed to enjoy it. I kept glancing around nervously in case Nelson had decided to catch the early show, but I didn't catch sight of his skinny shoulders hunched over a vat of popcorn, so I figured he'd taken the night off.

When the credits finally came up, Cam and I headed for the exit. He touched my arm and grinned. "You really let Arthur have it today," he said. "Although I have to say I agreed with you a hundred percent."

"Then why didn't you say anything?" I demanded, before I could stop myself. "All those Paramedics were staring at me as if I'd lost my mind. Okay, maybe I was a little tactless. But I'm starting to see how Minerva must feel. Sticking up for your principles can get a little lonely. And a little scary, too."

"You're right," he said. "Guess I didn't want to go out on a limb. I mean, those guys are in my sister's band. I have to put up with them around the clock. Know what I mean?"

I stared at Cam. "Yes, well, people will have to put up with Harvey Jenkins around the clock pretty soon too. Unless they crawl out on that limb a little farther."

Cam gave me an uncomfortable grin. "Ouch," he said.

Then he grabbed my hand and gave it a squeeze. "Okay," I said. "I forgive you. This time. Now, considering that you ate most of the popcorn, you can buy the pizza."

We headed out to the street. A block from the movie theater I caught Cam's arm. "Look," I said.

He turned to see what I was pointing at. A shabby-looking young guy sat on the steps of the post office. Next to him was a cardboard box. A homemade sign was propped next to it. FREE DOG, it said.

We stopped and looked in the box. Inside was a small, shivering black puppy. The man gave us an unhappy smile. "Got to split town," he said. "And I can't take little Molly with me."

"Why don't you take her to the animal shelter?" I asked. I felt so sorry for them. It was a cold evening, and the man and his dog both looked chilled.

He shrugged. "Too many pets in them places nowadays. She wouldn't stand a chance. Anyway, I figured if I sat here long enough, some kind folks might want her and I wouldn't have to have her put to sleep." He looked up at us hopefully.

"I'm sorry," I said. "But we already have a cat, and—"

Cam leaned forward decisively. "I'll take her," he said. He bent down and picked up the box. The puppy gave a whimper, and I petted her shaggy little coat. "But only on one condition," he added.

The man's relieved smile vanished. "What's that?" he said, his eyes darkening.

"You'll take ten dollars for her."

The man gulped and looked down at his sign.

"Final offer," Cam said firmly. "No sale, no dog."

"Well, if that's the way you want it," the man said tentatively, and I watched while Cam fished the money out of his pocket and handed it to Molly's owner.

"Good luck," he said.

With Cam carefully balancing the carton with the puppy inside, we headed down the street.

"That was our pizza money, wasn't it," I said.

"Yep," Cam answered. He gazed down at the shivering puppy.

"I'm glad you did it, Cam," I told him.

"Me too. You know, I think I'm starting to get the hang of this going-out-on-a-limb-business. I just hope my mom agrees."

Then Cam smiled and patted the dog's head. "I think I'll call her Pepperoni," he said, as we started up the hill.

eight

~~~~~~~~~~~~~~~~~~~~~~~~~~~~~~~~~~~~~~

Saturday morning I was just fixing a bowl of Frosted Flakes from my secret cache when my father strode into the room.

"Wash day," he announced. "I promised your mother I'd take care of things while she's steering this campaign, and I intend to keep that promise. So gather together all your dirty clothes and bring them down to the basement."

I went upstairs and dug out all the dirty clothes from the bottom of my closet. For good measure, I threw in Pru's blue sweater, which had one tiny little stain on the sleeve. I pushed all the clothes into the hamper until it was filled to the top and then hauled it all downstairs.

"Here," I said. "Are you sure you don't need any help?"

"Of course not," he said. "All I have to do is follow the directions your mother left. Which mainly seem to be, don't put the colored things in with the white things. And if you get confused, read the labels. Right?"

Dad scratched his beard and stared at the mountain of dirty clothes. He reached over and picked up a pink blouse. "This one says 'dry clean only,'" he said, holding up the label.

"It does?" I snatched the blouse out of his hands. "That can't be right," I said. I'd worn this blouse plenty of times and then thrown it in the hamper. "I guess you'd better wash it in cold water. And put in some Woolite, maybe."

"Right," he said. "Woolite. Fabric softener. Separate the colors. Read the labels. Find Mom's directions."

I gave him an encouraging smile. "Look at it this way. If Napoleon could run a whole army without Mom around, you can probably manage the laundry. If you need any help, just holler."

After a leisurely bowl of Frosted Flakes, I dialed Heather's number.

"Hi," I said, when she answered. "It's me. Are you still coming over tonight?"

Heather paused. "Well, yes and no," she said.

"Yes and no? What does that mean?"

"It means I have to baby-sit. My cousin Jenny usually sits for these people, but she has the flu. So she promised them she'd find someone. Anyway, she sort of volunteered me before I had a chance to turn it down."

Good old Jenny. "Well, okay, Heath," I said. "Even though I have tons of stuff to tell you . . ."

"Wait a minute." I could tell she was weakening. Then she said, "Why don't you come with me? Jenny said they live over in Magnolia. I bet it's one of those huge houses overlooking the Sound. They'll probably have tons of food and HBO and stuff."

I thought of the frozen eggplant Mom had left in the freezer for dinner. "Well, okay," I said. "They probably won't mind getting two sitters for the price of one."

"How about Pru? Does she want to come too?"

"I'll ask her," I said. "But I think she's got band practice."

"Whatever," Heather said. "My dad's going to drive me over there at six. We'll pick you up on the way."

Just as I hung up the phone, it rang again. It was my mother.

"Hi, sweetie," she said. "I'm over here at campaign headquarters. It looks like I'm going to be here pretty late. The mayor is giving a farewell gala for Ben Edwards tonight, and all the candidates are expected to show up."

She paused. "Oh, and remind your dad about the laundry," she said. "And see that he uses those instructions I left for him."

"Don't worry," I told her. "It's all taken care of. Listen, is it okay if I baby-sit with Heather tonight? She's filling in for her cousin Jenny for a family who live in Magnolia."

"That's fine," Mom said. "Just make sure your

father knows where you are and what time you'll be home. And listen—I appreciate the way you guys are keeping the home fires burning."

"Sure, Mom," I said. "Nothing to it!"

I went upstairs and found some clothes clean enough to wear. Then I decided to go next door and see how Pepperoni was settling into her new home.

Chloe greeted me at the door. "Isn't she adorable!" she exclaimed, ushering me into the kitchen. She pointed to the corner.

Cam sat in a chair. Wriggling in his arms was a fluffy little black bundle. He grinned up at me. "We just got back from the vet's. Peppy had a flea bath and a worm pill and all her shots. She's a certified mongrel, the doc says. Monday Dad's going downtown to get her a license."

I patted Pepperoni on her shiny little head. Her pink tongue lolled out, and she reached up and licked me on the hand. I totally melted.

"Dad says I can build her a dog house out in the backyard for when she's old enough. Right now, she's sleeping in my room."

"Well," I said, "I hope you keep a pile of newspapers in the corner. She's still pretty young."

Cam set her down on the floor. Peppy's tail was going so fast it looked as if it might wag right off her little body.

"Do you think they'd really have put her to sleep?" Chloe asked worriedly.

"Unless someone adopted her," Cam answered. "And who knows whether anyone would? That guy wasn't kidding. It's tough times for abandoned pets these days."

"And abandoned people," I added, thinking of that poor guy huddled on the cold steps of the post office. I hoped he had headed downtown to see Minerva's friend Bob at the First Avenue Mission. Spending the night in a shelter was no fun, I was sure, but it had to be better than the post office steps.

"It's just plain tough times, period," Chloe announced. "That's why it's so important to get the right people into office, so something can be done."

"Well, at least Peppy got lucky," Cam said. He ruffled her ears. "Hey, a new concept—recycled pets!"

I watched him play with the puppy. He looked so happy and proud. Then I thought about the dance; it was only a week away, and I hadn't said a word about it. To Cam or to Nelson.

Chloe came over and hugged me. "Don't they look cute together?" she said. I nodded, thinking that no one in her right mind would ever ask a boy to a dance with his mother right in the room.

"I was just about to make waffles," Chloe went on. "Can you stay and have some, Mattie?"

I looked at Cam. "Gee, I'd love to," I said, "but my father is doing the laundry, and I'd better get home in case he needs any help."

Chloe smiled. "Now, Mattie," she said. "Your father

has a Ph.D. I'm sure he'll do just fine on his own."

"All done," my father said proudly. John Darwin, Ph.D., held up the laundry basket, piled high with clean, freshly-folded clothes. "Actually," he said, "it really wasn't so hard. I should have taken over laundry duty years ago."

"Great job, Dad," I agreed.

"Thank you, Mattie. Why don't you put these away, and I'll start on the sheets and towels." Then he glanced at his watch and pretended to look surprised. "Good grief, it's almost time for lunch. I don't suppose you're in the mood for a pizza?"

He grinned and headed downstairs to order lunch. I was just thinking that I could have done a whole lot worse in the father department, when my pink blouse, which was folded on top of the pile, fell on the floor. As I leaned over to pick it up, I saw that one sleeve didn't look very pink anymore.

I held up the blouse. It definitely looked different. Less pink. And smaller. Much, much smaller.

I turned back to the basket and began pulling out more clothes. Pru's sweater was now big enough for a Barbie doll. Then I picked up a plaid dish towel. It took me a moment to realize it used to be my favorite pleated skirt.

"Mattie?" It was my father, coming back up the stairs. "I just ordered a ham and pineapple pizza. To tell the truth, I've always wondered what those tasted

76

like. You can pick off the pineapple if you don't like it."

I waited until he reached the bedroom door. Then I held up the Barbie doll blouse.

My father traced the outline of his beard with one forefinger. "It did say 'dry clean only,' Mattie," he reminded me. "I was only following *your* instructions."

"But you put them in the dryer, Dad! You're supposed to dry fine washables on a towel on the floor!"

He picked up Pru's tiny sweater. " 'Lay flat to dry,' " he read. "I laid it flat, inside the dryer. It doesn't say anything about a towel on the floor. I really think that sort of thing is open to interpretation."

"Pru's going to kill you, Dad."

He raised one eyebrow. "Us, Mattie. Pru's going to kill *us*."

By the time the Yamamotos picked me up, Pru and I were back on speaking terms. Mostly because I'd agreed to give her every sweater I ever bought for the rest of my life. I'd also invited her along on the baby-sitting job, but Pru reminded me that tonight was the night the winner would be announced on *Seattle Rocks*. The Paramedics were going to watch the show together at the Davises.

"I'll just die if we win," Pru said, and stifled a small scream. "Can you even imagine it? The Paramedics signing a contract with Lunar Records?"

"It's tough," I admitted. But I wished her luck.

Heather was leafing through a catalog of ecologically correct mail order products when I climbed into the backseat.

"Look," she said, pointing at a page. "Biodegradable balloons! These would be perfect for Minerva's campaign."

"Biodegradable. Does that mean they're edible?" Heather's father inquired.

"No, Dad," Heather said. "Although that isn't a bad idea."

I pictured little kids at birthday parties, munching on different flavored balloons. "Sure," I volunteered. "The red ones could be cherry, and the green ones lime." I paused. "Do you suppose there'd be much dietary fiber in edible balloons?"

No one had an answer for that.

"Okay," Heather said, as we pulled up in front of a big brick house. "This is it. 4131 Mockingbird Lane."

"Pretty fancy neighborhood," Mr. Yamamoto observed. He peered out at the other brick houses, each perched on top of a massive lawn. "You don't suppose their kids need music lessons, do you?"

"The Yankovics have one child, and she's four years old," Heather told him as she opened the car door. "She's also a spoiled brat, according to Jenny. But they pay their baby-sitters seven dollars an hour."

"Good," Mr. Yamamoto said. "That should just about cover the gas it took to drive you here."

"Relax, Daddy." Heather picked up her bookbag from the front seat. "Jenny said they always give her a ride home, and they never stay out late."

Mr. Yamamoto was still staring at the house. "I started you on the violin when you were only five," he said. "Never too soon to learn."

Heather sighed. "Okay, Daddy. I'll see what I can do."

As we started up the front walk to the house, I glared at a blue and yellow sign that was stuck in the front yard. HARVEY JENKINS FOR CITY COUNCIL — MAKE SEATTLE GREAT AGAIN!"

I poked Heather and frowned.

Heather gazed at the sign. "Come on, Mattie," she said. "It's only for a couple of hours."

"Well, okay. But it goes against my principles!"

Just as we reached the house, the garage door opened, and a Mercedes began to back down the driveway. I stared at the shiny blue car.

"That proves it," I said. "Definitely Harvey supporters."

Mrs. Yankovic was waiting at the front door. She was wearing a frilly pink dress and tons of jewelry. She glanced nervously at the man waiting in the Mercedes. "I'll be right out, dear," she called.

"I'm Judy Yankovic, and you must be Jenny's replacement," she said to Heather, and then gave me a nervous smile. "I was just frantic when Jenny said she couldn't make it. We have this important dinner tonight, and of course Elizabeth Anne is so fond of Jenny."

Mrs. Yankovic checked her watch. "Elizabeth Anne has had her dinner and bath, so all you have to do is tuck her in. There's snacks in the refrigerator if you get hungry. Oh, and the home alert system is on, so please don't open any of the doors and windows. Let's see, what else? I've left a number next to the phone where you can reach us, and—"

"Where's Jenny?" a high voice demanded. A little girl with curly blond hair stood in the middle of the living room. "I don't want *them*," she told her mother, pointing at us. "I want Jenny!"

"Now, Elizabeth Anne," the woman said nervously, "this is Jenny's cousin—"

"Heather," Heather put in. "And this is my friend Mattie."

"See, darling? You have two sitters tonight. Isn't that special?"

"I want Jenny!"

The car horn honked, and Mrs. Yankovic jumped. She leaned down to kiss Elizabeth Anne, who wriggled away. The woman sighed. "We won't be late," she told us. "And thanks again, girls. You're real lifesavers."

With a fluttery little wave, she ran down the steps to the waiting car, her high heels clicking on the flagstones.

Heather closed the front door. "Great," I said.

"Now you've activated the home alert system. We're sealed in here like mummies in a tomb."

"Mummy!" Elizabeth Anne began to shriek. "I want my mummy!"

I looked at Heather. "Guess it's time to start earning those seven dollars an hour. Meanwhile, I'm going to check out the refrigerator."

I left Heather telling Elizabeth Anne how much fun violin lessons were going to be, and strolled into the massive kitchen. Every surface was covered in fake Spanish tile. Even the refrigerator was adobe red. I wondered if the Yankovics had ever heard of Tijuana omelettes. Dad's cooking would definitely fit their decor.

I opened the door and stared at the bulging shelves. Heather would have a fit. Everything in the Yankovics' refrigerator was high calorie, high cholesterol, high caffeine, and loaded with added sugar. I could hardly wait to dig in.

I found a bowl in the next cupboard and helped myself to a mountain of fudge ripple ice cream, covered with aerosol whipped cream and caramel sauce. I was just finishing my second helping when Heather walked into the kitchen. She was mopping at her T-shirt with a towel.

"Elizabeth Anne threw up on me," she explained. "Then she fell asleep, so I put her to bed."

"I think these people are cheating you, Heather," I said. "Elizabeth Anne is definitely an eight-dollar-an-hour job. You'd better eat a lot of their ice cream."

I grabbed a napkin from the tiled kitchen table and was about to dab at Heather's shirt when I saw some gold writing on the napkin: VOTE FOR HARVEY JENKINS— HE'LL WIPE THE SLATE CLEAN!

"Can you believe this?" I said, waving the napkin at Heather. "There's Harvey magnets on the refrigerator, Harvey coasters in the living room. I'm scared to go into the bathroom in case they have 'Vote for Harvey' on the toilet paper."

Heather didn't answer. She was staring at some snapshots stuck on a bulletin board next to the phone.

"Mattie," she murmured. "Look at this."

"What is it?" I got up to fix myself another helping of ice cream. This time I'd try the gourmet fudge sauce, I decided.

Heather was pointing at a snapshot. It showed three people standing in front of a fishing boat. The name of the boat was the *Elizabeth Anne*. There, proudly pointing at a big salmon, was good old Harvey Jenkins. Standing next to him, one sleeve of a frilly pink sweater tucked possessively around his shoulder, was Mrs. Yankovic.

Heather and I looked at each other, as the awful possibility sank in.

"You don't suppose . . ." Heather began.

"Yes, Heather," I moaned. "That's exactly what I suppose. We're baby-sitting for Harvey Jenkins! Don't you see? That's why they needed a sitter in the first place. He and his wife must have gone to the mayor's reception for Ben Edwards!"

"Maybe it's not Harvey Jenkins," Heather said desperately. "I mean, maybe this one's his wife, and they're just friends of Mrs. Yankovic."

She pointed to the other woman in the picture, who had bright orange hair. It was the woman in polka dots I'd seen on the campaign truck that day at Nelson's.

"I don't think so, Heather," I said. "I mean, when you think about it, it's obvious—Yankovic . . . Jenkins. He probably figured he could sell more cars with a shorter name."

Heather looked miserable. "I'm sorry, Mattie. Jenny never said a word!"

"It's okay, Heather," I said. "But promise me you'll donate your baby-sitting money to a worthy cause. Like Minerva's campaign debt."

I handed her my bowl of ice cream. "I think I've lost my appetite. What did Marie Antoinette say during the French Revolution? Let them eat fudge ripple!"

"I think it was cake, Mattie," Heather said doubtfully. She looked down at the melting ice cream. There, staring up at us from the bottom of the bowl, were the words, "Vote for Harvey Jenkins, for a Sweeter Future."

Heather and I looked at each other. One thing was certain: we were deep in the heart of the enemy camp.

nine

~~~~~~

Some time later, we sat on the Yankovics' mile-long beige couch and wondered what to do.

"Come on, don't feel bad," I told Heather for the twentieth time. She was slumped against a pillow that said, "Vote for Jenkins, Not Higher Taxes." "Hey, how about another dish of ice cream? Or maybe some frozen yogurt. You have to admit they have good taste in snacks."

"No thanks," Heather said. She looked miserable. "I just feel so disloyal. I mean, the only reason we're here is so that Harvey Jenkins can go out and poison more minds!"

"They went to a banquet, Heather, not a book burning," I said, trying to cheer her up. "Besides, Minerva will be there too."

"So maybe we should have baby-sat her grandchildren instead," Heather said.

As usual, she had a good point. I looked down and spotted the remote control for the TV lying on the coffee table. "I know! It's almost time for *Seattle Rocks.*

We can see whether the Paramedics won the contest."

Heather perked up a little. "Okay," she said.

I flicked on the TV and found Channel 28. A bunch of kids were dancing energetically to loud music. Heather and I dissected their clothes and their hair and the way they were dancing. But it only reminded me of another unsolved problem.

I drew a deep breath, "Heather, you've got to help me. Should I ask Cam to the Sadie Hawkins dance? Or should I ask Nelson Richfield?"

I began chewing anxiously on my thumbnail. "I'd really rather go with Cam, I guess, but I know it would mean a lot to Nelson. And he probably won't go other-wise. In fact, I'm not sure if Nelson will ever go to a dance unless I ask him."

"You're probably right," Heather said, which didn't exactly help matters. "And I'm sure Cam will under-stand if you decide to ask Nelson. It's not as if no one else will ask him. There are plenty of girls who want to. Why, just the other day, Marcia Ames said—"

"Please, Heather," I groaned. "You're not making this any easier."

"Shh," Heather said. "The DJ's coming on."

The smiling man with the starched hair stood on a platform decorated with the *Seattle Rocks* logo. He held up a video cassette in one hand and an envelope in the other.

"All right, music fans of Seattle. This is the moment you've all been waiting for. In my hand is the name of the winner of our battle of the bands contest. For them, stardom is just a phone call away. For everybody else who entered, well . . ." He winked. "Let's just say, better luck next time. And keep practicing."

With a flourish, he handed the envelope to a woman with purple-streaked hair that stood up on top of her head. She bared her teeth at the camera and then ripped open the envelope.

Don't ask me why. But right then, even after all the unflattering stuff I'd said about the Paramedics, I really hoped they had won.

"And out of the four hundred entries we received, the winners are—the Frozen Doughnuts from Capital Hill!"

Immediately, the winning sounds of the Frozen Doughnuts filled the studio, while friends of the band let out shrieks of joy.

I turned down the volume. "They really don't sound any better than the Paramedics," I told Heather. "I hope Pru isn't going to be too upset."

"She shouldn't be. After all, it takes a lot of time and patience to have a musical career. You should hear my dad. He knows a lot of professional musicians, and he says—"

I turned and stared at her. "Heather! I just thought of something. Has your father ever heard the Paramedics play?"

"Sure. He heard them at the Golden Goat. He thought they were terrible."

"But that's not just because your dad doesn't like rock. It's because they don't know how to play." I was getting excited. "Let's face it, people aren't exactly showing up in droves to buy their kids violins. Are they?"

Heather ruefully shook her head.

"But you heard that woman just now—they got four hundred entries for this contest. That means a lot of kids in Seattle are trying to start their own bands."

Heather blinked at me. "So?"

"So, maybe Yamamoto Music should keep up with the times. I mean, opera's great and everything, but what about the kids? Maybe, instead of violins, your dad should start selling guitars and drums and electric pianos. And with every instrument, the kid could get a free lesson."

"Mattie, my dad doesn't know anything about rock music. How could he teach someone how to play the electric guitar or the drums?"

"Not your father, Heather. The professional musicians who come into his store. They'd probably be happy to get some students. And the parents would be happy, because the kids would actually know what to do with the stuff they buy. Look at Clark. Maybe if he could play more than one chord on the keyboards, the Paramedics would have done better."

Heather looked at me. "I don't know. Daddy's into Pavarotti, not Paramedics."

I sighed. "Yes, but I bet he could use the business.

Let's face it. Harvey Jenkins is a big success because he gives people what they want. So this way, your father could actually give the kids what they need at the same time."

I grabbed a pad of lined paper that was lying on the coffee table. "He could call it the Music Plus Plan." I scribbled it down on the pad. Then I wrote down a short list of my ideas, the way Mom did when she was making plans for the campaign. "Hey, once he has the kids coming into the store, who knows? He might get the parents interested in Pavarotti."

Heather looked at the Music Plus Plan. "Gee, Mattie. You know, it just might work."

I doodled a little treble clef on top of the pad. "Now, if only we can get Arthur and Zee to show up for some lessons."

I tore off the sheet of paper and handed it to Heather. But when I put the pad back on the table, something caught my eye. Then I looked closer, and I let out a little scream.

"What is it?"

"Oh, Heather . . . I don't believe this."

"Believe what?"

I pointed at the pad. "This," I whispered.

Scribbled on the top of the page were the words, "Plan to Develop Downtown Mission."

Underneath, in blue ink, was a list. It looked a lot like the Music Plus Plan, only shorter.

City raises rent on shelter, shelter can't pay,
city repossesses land.
Zoning commission??
Private development co. puts up condominiums,
property value increases?
Major profit potential.

The last three words were underlined.

Heather was squinting at the list. "What does it mean?"

"I don't know, for sure," I said. My voice was shaking. "But I can guess. Harvey's planning to get the city to turn the First Avenue homeless shelter into expensive apartment buildings. So that he—or someone he knows—can make a lot of money."

Heather looked shocked. "That's terrible, Mattie!"

I nodded slowly. "Yes, Heather. It sure is."

Then we just sat there, while in the background, the kids on *Seattle Rocks* danced furiously to the sounds of the Frozen Doughnuts.

A few hours later, Heather and I were still slumped on the couch, watching an old gangster movie. When the key turned in the lock, I half expected Edward G. Robinson to walk in, brandishing a machine gun.

Instead, there stood Harvey and Judy Yankovic.

"How was Elizabeth Anne? I hope she didn't give you any trouble," Mrs. Yankovic said anxiously.

Heather glanced down at the stain on her shirt. "She was fine," she said.

"Just great," I added. The pad with the list was back on the coffee table, hidden under a *TV Guide*. Mrs. Yankovic rushed down the hall to check on Elizabeth Anne. Harvey stood at the door, thumbing through his wallet.

"Let's see," he said, giving us his trademark grin. "I think this will cover your time and trouble." He whipped out two twenty dollar bills and handed them to us.

"I think that's too—" Heather started to say, but Harvey waved his hand grandly.

"Nonsense," he said. "Good baby-sitters are hard to find, especially at the last minute. And now, girls, if I may escort you outside, your chariot awaits."

I had to admit old Harvey could really lay on the charm. It probably came in handy selling luxury cars. We picked up our books and trooped outside to the Mercedes.

We sat silently in the backseat while the car whooshed through the city streets. The whole time Harvey carried on a loud conversation over his car phone. He didn't even pretend to lower his voice; he just acted as if he were alone in the car.

"I had them eating out of my hand, Dick," he said at one point. "I think we can pretty well call the shots. It's sewn up, I tell you. It's in the bag."

Harvey definitely had a way with clichés.

"Here you go, girls," he said finally, pulling up in front of Heather's house. "Now, don't forget, you tell Mom and Dad to come on down to the showroom and get a great deal on a family car. Well, an imported family car, anyway." He chuckled.

"Thank you, Mr. Jenkins . . . I mean, Mr. Yankovic," Heather said.

Harvey nodded jovially. He must have had a good time at the mayor's reception, I thought, staring at his tanned, crinkly face. And now he figured the election was in the bag. Soon he could take his seat on the council and start evicting homeless people from their shelter.

When we got out of the car, Harvey reached in his pocket again. I braced myself for another twenty, but instead he handed us each an Honesty in Politics windshield scraper.

"Hope Lizzie wasn't too much trouble," he said. "She can be a handful sometimes. Anyway, thanks again. You were real lifesavers."

With a majestic toot of the horn, the Mercedes pulled smoothly away from the curb and disappeared into the night.

Heather and I looked at each other.

"What are we going to do?" she asked me.

I glanced down at the windshield scraper in my hand. "I think it's time we put a little honesty back into politics, Heather," I said. "But first I'd better talk to Mom."

ten

~~~~~~~~~~~~~~~~~~~~~~~~~~~~~~~~~~~~

When I opened my eyes on Sunday morning, I tried to remember the weird dream I had just had. It was all about pretending to be a baby-sitter, and spying on Harvey Jenkins, and finding a horrible secret that turned out to be the takeout menu from a Chinese restaurant.

Then I remembered that it wasn't a dream. The horrible-secret part, anyway.

When I got downstairs, I peered into the kitchen. Half a dozen pizza boxes were stacked next to the garbage pail. Dad must have ordered every variety he'd ever dreamed of.

I was just about to take them outside when the kitchen door opened and Sally walked in, yawning.

"Morning, sweetie," she said. I watched her go over to the stove and start the kettle for her herb tea.

"Hi, Mom. How did the gala go?"

"From all reports, it was a nice evening. Minerva said everyone was cordial to each other. For the sake of Ben Edwards, anyway."

She yawned and reached into the cupboard for the tea canister. "But just so you don't feel left out, Minerva's invited the whole family over tonight for a little campaign celebration. To reward everybody for living on frozen casseroles all this time."

I paused, the stack of pizza cartons hidden behind my back. I put them down next to the door and walked over to where Sally was shaking tea into the strainer.

"Mom," I said, "I have a terrible confession to make."

She looked startled. "You do?" Then her glance swept over to the door, and a little smile crooked at the corners of her mouth. "If it's about not eating that eggplant casserole, I guess I can find it in my heart to forgive you."

I swallowed. "No, it isn't that." I paused. "Last night, Heather and I baby-sat for Harvey Jenkins."

Sally stood quietly, holding the tea. She gave me a questioning look.

"I mean, we didn't know it was Harvey's house until we got over there. His real name is Yankovic. Anyway, the thing is . . ."

As the kettle began to whistle, I watched Sally make her tea while I told her about the pad of paper and the words I'd seen on it. "It was an accident, honest! I picked up this pad—and there it was. Harvey's master plan to turn the downtown mission into luxury condos!"

My mother took a sip of her tea. "Well, Mattie, to

use a campaign expression, that is what is commonly known as political dynamite. The question is—is it fair to light it?"

"But, Mom," I practically yelled, "how can you ignore something like that? Don't the voters have a right to know what's going to happen if they elect Harvey Jenkins?"

Sally took her tea over to the kitchen table. "Honey, that's the problem with dynamite. Sometimes it can blow up in your face. All Harvey has to do is deny everything, and then it's Minerva who will have to defend herself. Not Harvey."

"But that isn't fair!" I thought about Harvey's latest commercials, the ones that called Minerva everything from an environmental terrorist to a dangerous radical. I just couldn't understand it. How come the good guys—or women—always finished last?

"I could testify under oath that I saw it. You should have heard him on the way home, Mom. He spent the whole time talking on his car phone about how he had the election all sewn up. I mean, aren't we entitled to unravel it?"

Sally took another sip of tea. "I'll mention this to Minerva tonight," she said. "The election's only three days away, and frankly, we haven't done that well in the polls. It's possible that something like this might galvanize people. But first we'd have to prove it."

"Maybe you could find out who this development

company is," I said. "What about talking to the people who run the mission? Even if you can't catch Harvey, there might be a way to stop him before he does anything."

Sally gave me a thoughtful nod. Then she said, "Not bad, Mattie. If I didn't know you better, I'd say you had a little political fever in your genes."

I shrugged. It embarrassed me when Mom made a big deal out of things. "Just a late bloomer," I said.

Sally grinned. "Ah, but blood will tell." Then she looked over at the pizza cartons. "Or, in the case of your father, cholesterol will tell."

"Cholesterol will tell you what?"

Pru stood in the doorway. She was wearing a ratty old bathrobe, and I could tell from her red-rimmed eyes that she'd been crying.

That's when I remembered the contest. Poor Pru. She'd been all ready to design the album cover for Lunar Records' first Paramedics release. And then, disaster struck in the form of the Frozen Doughnuts.

"It looks like Dad really went nuts with the pizza last night," I remarked.

"That was for the band," Pru said. She shuffled over to the refrigerator and took out a pitcher of juice. "But I didn't eat any of it. I was too upset. Those horrible Doughnuts!" Angrily Pru poured herself a glass of orange juice and gulped it down. "They just won because they're friends of the DJ. Everybody says so."

"Now, Prudence Darwin. Those are sour grapes if I ever heard them." Sally gazed sternly at Pru. "If the winning band had those kinds of connections, why even bother to hold a contest?"

Pru opened her mouth to make another snappy comeback. The next second, her face had crumpled up, and she sank down in a chair like a sad little lump.

Sally nudged me. "Come on, Pru," I said, kneeling down by her chair. "Maybe you need some new material. Maybe 'Terror in the Night' just wasn't your breakthrough song."

"But it was our best one!" Pru wailed. "We spent all this time getting it perfect, and then the stupid Frozen Doughnuts had to win. And they didn't even need to. They already play all over the place!"

Sally put her arm around Pru. "Honey, it's just possible that that's why they won. They probably had a little bit more experience than Zee and the boys. Look on the bright side—if you guys stick with it, you'll get there too."

"Oh, Mom! You sound like a football coach or something." Pru wiped her eyes on the sleeve of her robe. "Now you'll tell me that a winner never quits."

"Nope. In my opinion, a loser never quits. Until she becomes a winner. The main thing is to be patient. If you go back to the drawing board enough times, you'll get it right. I promise."

"Mom?" I asked. "What if Minerva doesn't win?

Does that mean you'll go back to the drawing board too?"

Sally nodded. "Yep. I don't know if that will mean another campaign. But I think if you work hard to make people aware of things like pollution and poverty and AIDS, change will come. You just can't give up. Right, Pru?"

"I guess so." Pru heaved a sigh. Then she brightened. "Maybe it's that dumb tambourine. Do you think I could get a guitar, Mom? I'd practice and everything, honest."

This time it was Mom who heaved a sigh. She patted Pru's shoulder. "We'll see, sweetie."

That reminded me of my Music Plus idea. For a moment I thought of telling Mom and Pru about it. Then I figured I'd better give Heather a call first. I headed for the phone in the living room.

I stopped when I reached the door.

The floor was covered with towels. They were spread over practically every inch of carpet, and each one held a blouse or sweater carefully laid out flat to dry.

I went over to one of the towels, where Dad had attempted to stretch Pru's sweater into a recognizable shape. It was still awfully Barbie-sized, but the sleeves looked quite a bit longer now. I wondered if chimpanzees ever wore sweaters.

For a moment I gazed down at the damp blouses and

sweaters that were spread out like a miniature battle-field around the living room. Then, quietly, I climbed the stairs to the Black Hole.

I swept the sleeves of Mom's silk blouse out of my face and gave a little cough. Dad looked up from his typewriter.

"Hey, we're all invited over to Minerva's tonight. Who knows? Maybe she's making chicken-fried steak."

"Good," Dad said, "I'm hungry. Those friends of Pru's didn't leave much in the way of dinner last night. Six pizzas gone in thirty seconds. I've seen a tank of piranhas take longer." He gave me a distracted pat on the shoulder and turned back to his typing.

"Oh, and Dad? Thanks for doing the laundry, again." I paused. Then I added, "But you really didn't have to. I mean, the whole thing was my fault. I should have followed the directions better."

Dad studied me for a moment. Then he smiled.

"Actually, Mattie, I think it was my fault. Trial and error doesn't apply to laundry." He scratched his beard. "And they don't apply to cooking either. Just because your mother pretended to like it, all those years ago."

"Well, she was falling in love with you, Dad," I pointed out. "And you know something? I bet if you made one of those fire omelettes right now, Mom would *still* pretend she liked it."

My father looked at me quizzically. "You think so, Mattie?"

I nodded. "She told me she used to love every bite."

"Well, what do you say we find out?" And before I could utter another word, Dad was out the closet door, and heading down the stairs to make my mother a breakfast she would never forget.

As I followed him down to the kitchen, I thought of those TV commercials that told people to "say it with flowers." I was starting to figure out that people said it with different things. My father said it with Tabasco sauce. Cam said it with gory movies. Pru said it by lending me her sweaters, even if she was grumpy about it afterward.

Yes, I thought, as I heard the sound of eggs cracking on the side of a bowl, sometimes love had absolutely nothing to do with flowers.

eleven

~~~~~~~~~~~~~~~~~~~~~~~~~~~~~~~~~~~~

Minerva Hightower lived in the north end of town, in a big, comfortable house with wide steps leading up to a front porch. I followed Pru up the steps and into the kitchen, which wasn't nearly as color-coordinated as Harvey Jenkins's but smelled deliciously of garlic and butter and Italian herbs.

Minerva's husband, Frank, stood in the kitchen stirring a big pot of sauce. He was a jolly-looking man, wearing an apron and a big white chef's hat; I couldn't decide whether the hat was a joke or not, but I instantly got the feeling that Frank "said it" with food. Dad hustled over and began discussing the proper way to simmer spaghetti sauce.

The house was full of people—Minerva's campaign workers and their families. Minerva gave each of us a hug as she swept around the living room. "I didn't want to wait for election night to have the party," she explained, as she gave me a quick, perfume-scented squeeze. "If we win, people will be too excited to do anything but scream and yell. And if we lose—well, there's nothing like a concession speech to make the champagne go flat."

After every piece of garlic bread was consumed and every strand of spaghetti was gone, I wandered into the library at the back of the house. A baby grand piano stood in front of the windows. There was a fireplace with pictures of some little kids on the mantel—they must be Minerva's kids or maybe grandchildren. All around the room were bookshelves, filled to the ceiling.

You can tell a lot about people from their books. I pictured Harvey Jenkins's house and how there had only been some sports and business magazines and paperback romance novels sprinkled around. Harvey and his wife were probably people who didn't have much time to read, and when they did, they didn't really care what it was.

Minerva Hightower, on the other hand, seemed to care a lot about books. For one thing, she had all kinds—classics, poetry, biographies, best sellers—and you could tell she took good care of them. My parents have lots of books too, but over the years they've fallen apart, or gotten lost, or Pru and I have gotten into them and spread peanut butter between the pages. But Minerva's books were as beautiful and tempting as candy in a store window.

I ran a finger over some gleaming leather bindings. I wanted to pull each book off the shelf and curl up in a corner of the sofa and spend the next year just reading.

Then my hand froze. I stared down at a framed picture that stood in the corner of one of the bookshelves. It showed two little girls, exactly alike. They were wearing sailor suits. As I stared at their identical faces, I felt as though I was standing next to Pru and we were looking in a mirror.

"It must seem familiar, Mattie. It is Mattie, isn't it?"

Minerva was leaning on the piano, smiling down at me. "I bet you didn't know I had a twin sister, did you?"

"Does she live in Seattle?"

Minerva laughed. "No, she lives in Chicago with her family. She's a teacher. Her name's Miranda." She made a face. "I envy you and your sister, having such different names. Most parents can't resist giving their twins something with the same letter, or even names that rhyme. I don't think they realize how much ammunition that gives to the people who don't want to tell twins apart."

I stared back at the picture of the two smiling faces. Minerva a twin! I just couldn't get over it.

"That's me on the right." She pointed at herself, at the girl with the slightly rounder face, her eyes a little more tilted than her sister's. "We grew up in Chicago. Then our family moved out here, but Miranda went back to Chicago to go to college, and our lives moved off in different directions. But I call her almost every week. Because, in a funny way, we're still a part of each other."

102

There were so many questions I wanted to ask. Was it hard, leaving Miranda? Did you ever fight over the same boy? Did you have to share a room when you were growing up? Did you ever wish you weren't a twin? Did you ever stop feeling like one?

But I didn't have the nerve. So I just smiled at Minerva and put the picture back on the shelf. I felt shy, all of a sudden, as if I'd stumbled on a personal secret.

A little while later, when Pru came in, I showed her the picture of Minerva and her twin.

Pru studied the picture in silence. "I wonder," she said finally. "If Minerva and her twin had married twins, technically their children would be siblings wouldn't they?"

Minerva nodded. "You know, I never thought about that before, Pru. I'm afraid it's a little too late for that now, though."

Pru looked at me. "Maybe Mattie and I will marry twin brothers," she said. "Just think—a huge, extended family, all from the same gene pool!"

Personally, I couldn't imagine anything worse than starting a big identical dynasty. I looked over at Minerva. Maybe she knew of a good college in Chicago that I could apply to before Pru started digging up twin brothers to marry.

On the way home, I asked Mom if she'd told Minerva about Harvey's condo plan.

"Yes, Mattie. Tomorrow she's going to talk to the

people at the shelter and find out if there's any way they can extend their agreement with the city. In the meantime, I'm going to make a few phone calls and see if Harvey has any other sweetheart deals under way." Sally shook her head. "I have a feeling we've seriously underestimated our opponent."

"Your opponent's greed, you mean," I added.

Sally smiled. "Well, that's one way of putting it," she said. "But you have to understand, most people running for office represent the interests of one group or another. Sure, candidates have to appeal to the greatest number of voters to get elected, but it's not unusual for them to promise certain things to make sure they get the right amount of support."

"You mean, like Minerva belonging to environmental groups and the Women's Coalition? But that's right on her brochure! I don't think Harvey exactly announced he was going to kick homeless people out on the street to help some real estate developer."

We were stopped at a red light. My father glanced across the backseat. "Unfortunately, Mattie, that's not exactly unusual either. Some politicians don't want people to know about the deals they've made. They say one thing and do another. And once they've won, there isn't much the voters can do about it."

"Like the Frozen Doughnuts," Pru muttered.

Dad stared at her. "What?"

"The band that won the *Seattle Rocks* contest," Pru said. "First Mom says that they must have won fair and square, even though they're friends with the people on the show. Then you turn around and say that politicians make all these secret deals and promises so that they can get elected. So who am I supposed to believe?"

My parents exchanged looks. Dad sighed. "Prune, I'm glad you asked that question. I think this one's yours, Sal."

My mother shifted uncomfortably. "Pru," she began, "I'm not saying the world is a perfect place. Or that people are perfect. Politics can get very dirty, which is one reason Minerva decided to run for office. To prove that you can be honest and stand for the right things and still get your message across. I guess all I'm saying is that the world is full of both Minervas and Harveys . . ."

"And Frozen Doughnuts," I added helpfully.

". . . and it's up to you to decide which kind of person you want to be."

"But Mom," Pru said. "What happens if the Minervas don't win? I mean, what chance do the rest of us have then?"

There was silence in the car. Finally I said, "But she will win, won't she, Mom? Because we'll just have to move away if Harvey Jenkins gets elected! I'll refuse to live here!"

"Whoa." Dad held up one hand. "Not so fast. We're not moving until the mortgage is paid off, Harvey or no Harvey. Besides, where do you plan to go?"

"I'll to go Canada," I said desperately, "like people

did in the sixties. I'll find a nice Canadian family that will take me in, until things improve around here. Sure, it might be a little cold up there, and I'd have to get used to using different money, and singing 'O Canada' at the baseball games, but—"

"Nice try." My father pulled into the driveway and set the handbrake. Then he turned around and said firmly, "After all the trouble I went to, moving my desk out of a perfectly good office and into your mother's closet, I forbid you to move to Canada. Is that clear, Matilda?"

Matilda. Dad meant business. I nodded.

But as we started up the front steps, Mom put her arm around me. "Don't worry, Mattie. You won't have to move away. Everything's going to be just fine, you'll see."

"Sure, Mom," I said. Then I paused. "Hey, did you know that Minerva is a twin?"

"A twin? No, Mattie, I didn't. I know she has a sister in Chicago, but . . . a twin? Well, what do you know." And she smiled and ruffled my hair.

That night, I lay in bed thinking about Minerva and her twin. How they'd gone off and lived in different places and had jobs and families and met hundreds of people who didn't think of them as Minerva and Miranda. Someday, I figured, Pru and I would go off on our own too.

Maybe Pru would be a famous musician and travel

all over the world, and I'd be the one who got married—to nobody who immediately came to mind, of course—and have a lot of kids, and maybe run a restaurant and manage campaigns in my spare time.

Or maybe we'd both move away and have interesting careers and do exciting things. But we'd call each other every week, I figured. And whenever I needed some grumpy advice, or a shoulder to cry on, or even just an extra sweater, I had the feeling Pru would always be there. And I'd be there for her.

Whether we liked it or not.

twelve

~~~~~~

On Monday, I called an emergency lunchtime meeting of the Puget Sound Academy Political Action Committee—Cam, Nelson, and Heather.

"This is it," I said. "The eleventh hour. We've got to do something."

Nelson flicked his hair. "No kidding," he said. "All we've got for our documentary so far is you guys stuffing envelopes. I don't think Briggs is going to consider that standing on the sidelines of history. Sitting, maybe. But it's not enough."

"Hey, come on," Cam protested. "I got some great shots of my mom handing out leaflets downtown. Really, it's good stuff."

"Hold it!" I said. "I'm not talking about our project. I am talking about the election for city council. Harvey Jenkins must be stopped!"

Nelson peered at me. "What do you suggest, Darwin? Renting a bulldozer and leveling Jenkins Quality Imports?"

"Not exactly. But you said it yourself—we've got to fight fire with fire. It's time Minerva went on the offensive."

"Maybe we should organize something." Heather spoke so softly I almost didn't hear her.

"Organize something? Like what?"

Heather took a sip of milk. Then she wiped her mouth carefully and said, "What about a rally for the shelter? To get people to come and support Minerva's campaign. And maybe they could bring something for the food bank while they were at it. Instead of making a campaign contribution, they could donate a can of food."

Nelson began nodding enthusiastically. "Definitely telegenic, Yamamoto," he said. "I like it."

I stared at him while he was dipping his hand into my bag of potato chips. "Nelson, could you please explain something to me? Why do you always call girls by their last names? You call me Darwin. You call Heather Yamamoto. Is there something about our first names you don't like?"

Nelson didn't say anything, but his face turned red, and he hastily pushed my potato chip bag away.

"I think I know why," Cam said a little while later, as we were walking down the hall together. "It's so that he can forget you guys are girls."

"But what's wrong with being a girl?" I demanded.

Cam laughed. "Nothing," he said. "Besides, I think

it's kind of cute. Maybe I'll call you Darwin from now on. Except that I'd have to start calling your sister Darwin too."

"No, really, Cam—what's Nelson's problem with girls?"

Cam stopped in the middle of the hall. "Do I really have to answer that question?" he said.

"Oh," I said. Nelson's problem was ... Nelson. "No, I guess not."

We started walking again, bumping shoulders a little, and I was just beginning to relax when Cam gave me a nudge.

"Is that some kind of school tradition or something?" He was pointing at a poster for the Sadie Hawkins dance. It showed a cartoon of a cavewoman dragging a helpless young caveman off by the hair.

"What? Oh, you mean, the dance?"

Cam nodded.

"Oh, well, sort of. It just means the girls get to invite the boys, instead of the other way around." I laughed nervously. "Didn't they have those down in California?"

"Yeah, I guess so."

My hands felt cold and clammy. Was he waiting for me to invite him? I looked at Cam. Then I looked at the poster. "Well? Do you think you'd like to go?"

"Can't say. No one's asked me."

I looked down at the linoleum floor. "Not even Marcia Ames?"

Cam laughed. It was a really loud laugh, and a few other kids walking down the hall turned and stared at us. "No, not even Marcia Ames," he said.

"Well . . ." I peeked up at him. "Would you like to? Go, that is? With, er, me?"

Cam smiled. "Sure," he said. "Thanks, Darwin. I think that would be fun."

Later, when I got home, I was surprised to see Heather's mother sitting at the kitchen table, drinking a cup of tea with my mother. Usually Mrs. Yamamoto was at work during the day at her brother's import shop.

"Hi, Mattie," my mother greeted me. "Emiko was just telling me about the rally. She said you kids came up with the idea. I think it's wonderful."

"You do?"

"Yes," Sally said. "I especially like the part about the food donation. That really brings the focus back to where it belongs—people who have nowhere else to go."

She turned to Mrs. Yamamoto. "Chloe and I decided we'd bring some stuff down from the Golden Goat and really make a statement about feeding the hungry. Would you be willing to be in charge of hot drinks?"

I put my books down on the table. "When is all of this happening?" I asked.

"The sooner the better." Sally jumped up and headed for the phone. "In fact, let me give Bev at the

Queen Anne Gazette a call right now. I can count on her to get some media people over there tonight."

"Tonight?"

Mrs. Yamamoto smiled at me. "Tomorrow's the election, you know. This is really our last chance to get something going."

Tomorrow! "Mom? Do you think it would be all right if I brought some kids from school to the rally tonight?"

Sally smiled. "Well, sure, Mattie. But it would be even better if they brought their parents along."

Then, off in the distance, I heard an electronic squawk. "Let's make Seattle great again!" a voice howled, as Harvey's campaign truck rolled through the neighborhood.

I looked back at Sally and Mrs. Yamamoto. As far as I was concerned, we were past the eleventh hour, and we didn't have a moment to waste.

At five-thirty, Nelson hopped out of his mother's car. He was carrying a huge megaphone.

"Nelson," I said, when he reached the front porch, "do you really think that's going to be necessary?"

He looked down at the megaphone. "You never know, Mattie. The PA system might go out during Minerva's speech. Doesn't hurt to be prepared."

Nelson looked flushed and excited, and I noticed that for once he hadn't called me Darwin. I sat him down on the porch with instructions not to move. Then I went off to find Pru.

She was nowhere in sight. When I called Heather, I found out that she had already gone to the shelter with her mother, to set up a table of hot coffee and cocoa.

Back on the porch, Nelson was still sitting on the steps, making trombone noises through his megaphone. He looked up at me, and I felt a sudden pang of guilt. The Sadie Hawkins dance was probably Nelson's one and only chance to start a normal social life, away from postal chess and tending his aquarium and preparing for a lonely career as a scientific genius. I would just have to explain this to Cam and hope that he'd understand. "Nelson?" I said.

Just then, a car pulled into the driveway and Chloe beeped her horn. "Your mom's over at the Goat loading food. I told her I'd cart you kids down to the rally," she called. "Ready?"

"Or not," I said, and I followed Nelson down to the car.

Cam was studying something when we piled into the backseat. It was a book called *The Expert's Guide to Shooting Home Videos*. He glanced over at Nelson and his megaphone, nodded, and then turned back to his book.

Chloe headed downtown. "Oh, I'm so excited about tonight! I did Minerva's chart this morning, and all her aspects point toward success. Minerva has a Leo sun with Scorpio rising. That's a very powerful combination."

"But what if Harvey's a Leo too?" Nelson asked.

"I checked," Chloe said confidently. "Harvey's a Gemini. Take it from me," she added, glancing over her shoulder, "this is *not* his month!"

A crowd of people was already gathered at the First Avenue Mission. I gazed around at the historic brick buildings that surrounded Pioneer Square. I'd been down here before to take the Underground Seattle tour with my dad, but it looked different now—the soft glow from the antique lampposts was outstripped by dozens of TV lights trained on the front of the shelter.

A makeshift podium was set up on the steps, and people—some volunteers, some just curious—were milling around several huge barrels, brimming with food donations.

Cam was eyeing the camera crew. "Let me out here," he told his mom. "I want to ask those guys a couple of questions."

"Why don't I drop you girls off too?" Chloe said. "I'll grab a parking spot and catch up with you in a second," she added, just as Sally came rushing up.

"There you are!" she exclaimed when she saw Nelson and me. Then she frowned. "Where's your sister?"

"Pru?" I said. "I thought she was with you!"

A stricken look crossed Sally's face.

"It's okay, Mom," I said. "She's probably off somewhere with Arthur and his father, learning how to sell real estate."

Sally grimaced. Then she turned and gazed at the crowd. "Hey, isn't this great? Let me go find Minerva. I think she's about ready to make a statement."

The crew from *NewsCenter 4* had set up their cameras and lights near the podium. Nelson and I found Cam getting some advice on zoom shots from one of the cameramen. A line of shabby-looking men were lined up for hot coffee poured by volunteers wearing Minerva Hightower for a Change buttons, and I saw reporters with their pencils poised, waiting for Minerva to begin her speech.

Finally she stepped up to the microphone and tapped it. The amplifier gave a loud squeak. The crowd on the steps of the shelter quieted.

"Thank you all for being here," Minerva began. "Tomorrow is an important day for Seattle voters. I know it won't be an easy choice for many people, but I can guarantee it will be a clear one. As you know, my campaign slogan is about change. As you also know, change doesn't come easily or painlessly. Or cheaply." Laughter rippled through the crowd.

"While we're on the subject," Minerva continued, "let's talk about money."

I felt a hand on my shoulder, and looked up to see Mom standing behind me. She gave me a quick squeeze and then nodded toward Minerva.

"My opponent, Mr. Jenkins, has made many promises to the people of this city. Promises about lowering taxes, about slashing budgets while still improving our schools and services. All I can say is—Harvey, let's give those promises a test drive before we buy them!"

That brought a bigger laugh, and a smattering of applause.

When the laughter stopped, Minerva's voice grew serious. "So, what am I doing on the steps of this shelter, a place where our neediest citizens come when they need a meal, a bed, a blanket? After all, these are people who aren't worried about taxes, because they don't have incomes. They aren't too concerned about moorage fees at the marinas, because they don't own boats. Or cars, or sometimes anything at all. As a matter of fact, these people often don't even vote. So why should a candidate for political office care about them?"

"Because we're people too!" a man in the crowd shouted, and I saw that it was Pepperoni's owner, the guy Cam and I had seen huddled in front of the post office. "Believe me," he added, "I'd like to vote, lady. But it's tough to register when you can't give them no address."

Minerva nodded and faced the rest of the crowd. "This mission is an address, though, isn't it? And it's been here for forty years. But it may not be here for forty more. Not, as I hope, because someday all people will have enough to eat and a roof over their heads, but because the Octopus Group wants to raze the building

116

and put up condominiums. And who do you suppose is part of this group? My opponent, Harvey Jenkins, that's who!"

There was a buzz among the reporters, and the cameras moved closer to the podium. Minerva held up a piece of paper. "I am holding a copy of their prospectus. It's all here in black and white. You won't find it on any campaign brochure, I assure you. But I've met with the mayor, and I'm hopeful that a long-term lease can be worked out with—"

"I protest this charade!"

A man walked up and glared at Minerva. "My name's Richard Smithers. I'm a limited partner in the Octopus Group, and I don't think the business dealings of private citizens are any business of yours, Mrs. Hightower. Furthermore, I don't think you'll find the name Jenkins anywhere in that prospectus. In fact, we are considering slapping you with a lawsuit!"

"That's just fine, Mr. Smithers," Minerva said smoothly. "In fact, I think it's a wonderful idea. Let's get all this dirty dealing out in the open, where the people of the city can make up their own minds about it."

Nelson poked me. "You have to admit, she's got guts," he said.

"What's a limited partner?" I whispered.

"Shh, I'll explain it to you later," Nelson whispered back.

Just then, Heather ran over, and the three of us

moved closer to the steps, while Cam wove through the crowd with his videocam.

"I demand to know who's leaking this information," the man went on. "If you're so open-minded, let's hear who your sources are."

The buzzing of the reporters stopped. Everyone turned to look at Minerva. "Well?" the man said angrily.

All of a sudden I felt Heather grip my hand. At the same moment I pictured the headlines: BABY-SITTER STUMBLES ON CONDO PLAN: ELECTION DECLARED ILLEGAL. Or even: TOTGATE SCANDAL STUNS CITY.

"Well?" the man said again.

Then, out of the vacuum of silence, I heard a familiar voice rise above the Pioneer Square traffic. It was high and slightly nasal, and it was coming from somewhere to my left. It was Nelson's.

He aimed his megaphone at the podium. "Aren't investment offerings supposed to be available for the public to examine? Why, I bet anybody who wanted to could go down to the records department and find out all kinds of stuff. Besides," Nelson went on, his voice booming through the big red cone, "a kid in my class told me that Harvey Jenkins isn't really the guy's name. It's Yankovic, isn't it? Maybe that's what's on the prospectus."

"You're absolutely right," Minerva answered. I spotted a twinkle in her eye. "Mr. Jenkins—a name

Mr. Yankovic uses only for his public dealings—has quite a number of other business interests too. All filed down at the Public Administration Building. Open Monday through Friday." She smiled broadly.

A reporter standing next to us looked over and grinned at Nelson. "There's a source for you, Dick," he called to Mr. Smithers, whose face had turned bright red. "Why don't you start serving subpoenas on the local junior high?"

A relieved wave of laughter swept through the crowd. Minerva began talking about the good work that the shelter was doing, about the day-care center that was being planned and the job training program. The man from the Octopus Group hastily slipped away.

I looked over at Nelson, wanting to thank him, wanting to tell him that he was the one who had guts. But he wasn't looking at me. He was watching some people unloading objects from a nearby van.

I followed his gaze. And then I saw something that made me wish I hadn't. There, unpacking his drum kit, was Arthur Boyle. And there was Pru. The Paramedics had arrived!

thirteen

Everyone agreed it was an incredibly successful rally. After the speeches, the Paramedics, dressed in matching purple sweatshirts, played a twenty minute set, and even though they didn't have the polish—or maybe the glaze—of the Frozen Doughnuts, no one seemed to mind. Except for Mr. Yamamoto, who signed up Zee Davis for his Music Plus Plan on the spot (saxophone plus voice lessons, all at one low monthly cost).

A few of the reporters hung around to listen to the band and have coffee and doughnuts, but most of them left immediately after Minerva's announcement to go file their stories.

Minerva stood beside the food bank barrels, shaking hands and distributing campaign flyers. Bob Kelly, the shelter's director, was elated at all the donations, not to mention the press coverage. "Maybe this will open a few eyes," he told us.

"And hearts," Sally put in.

"And wallets," Nelson finished.

Heather kept giving Nelson awestruck glances. "I couldn't believe you spoke up like that," she told him. "Weren't you scared?"

Nelson tried to look suave, by leaning nonchalantly on his megaphone, and failed miserably. "Nah," he said. "I knew no one was going to turn you guys in. I just wanted to make a point. Freedom of information. The public's right to know."

My mother was listening. "Well, you did the right thing, Nelson," she said. "You all did. And maybe if this story makes the late news, we'll see some votes changed. But first," she said, "I've got some hungry mouths to feed." And she made her way over to the table where Chloe was dishing up bowls of vegetarian chili.

Nelson and I got some chili and sat down on the steps to eat. "You really were great, Nelson," I said, between bites. "You should have seen the look on that guy's face. I thought he was going to explode when you got to the part about Harvey's name."

Nelson chewed thoughtfully on a piece of corn bread. "That's another thing," he remarked. "Why do so many people assume kids are useless twerps? Why, I bet you and I could do a much better job than half the people on that council. Teamwork. That's the name of the game."

The moment had come; I couldn't put it off any longer. I put down my chili and faced Nelson. "Nelson," I said, my voice quaking a little, "has anyone asked you to the Sadie Hawkins dance yet?"

Nelson frowned. He took another bite of corn bread and stared at me. "Darwin," he said, "what on earth are you talking about?"

I took a deep breath. "Nelson, I'm asking you to go to the eighth-grade dance with me on Friday. Dance. That's where they play music and kids move around in time to it? You must have heard of those. It's sort of a quaint custom?"

Nelson chewed slowly, thinking it over. "Ah, the dance on Friday," he said finally, as if it had just occurred to him. "Are you sure I'm not supposed to ask you?"

"This is a Sadie Hawkins dance. The girls ask the boys. I'm asking you. Do you want to go or not?" I could feel a wave of impatience starting to overtake my noble gesture.

Nelson examined a crumb on his knee. "Yes," he said. "I guess I'd be willing to be your guest at the dance, Darwin. If it would really mean that much to you, I'll go."

Good old Nelson. Somehow, I hadn't expected him to act as if he were doing me a big favor. When I was the one who—

I stopped myself. If I was really going through with this, I had to stop feeling sorry for Nelson. I straightened and looked him square in the eye.

"Not a guest, Nelson. A date. That's what you call it when you go to a dance with someone. And furthermore, I'll only go with you on two conditions. One, you stop calling me Darwin. It makes me feel like a private in the army or something. And two, that you dress appropriately for the occasion."

Nelson raised an eyebrow. "Meaning?"

"Meaning that you make your mom take you to Wyndham's Tyger Department and buy you something decent to wear. Something cool. Presentable. Fashionable. Look in a magazine, for crying out loud!"

Nelson studied me with mild interest. "This reminds me of *My Fair Lady*," he said. "You know, when Henry Higgins wants to take Eliza to the ball and pass her off as a princess."

I picked up my chili. It was cold, but I ate some anyway. "Don't worry, Nelson," I said finally. "No one's asking you to pass yourself off as a princess. Or even a prince."

"That's a relief," Nelson said, and we finished our chili in silence. But I couldn't help noticing that Nelson seemed pretty pleased with himself. Maybe it was just the way he was humming under his breath. Probably the overture to *My Fair Lady*.

And, even though I was probably the only girl in the eighth grade who had asked two boys to the Sadie Hawkins dance, I had to admit the look on Nelson's face was worth it.

Well, almost worth it.

On the way home, I sat between my unsuspecting dates for the dance, praying that neither of them would bring it up. Luckily, Cam spent most of the ride raving over the great footage he'd gotten of Minerva and Nelson and the Paramedics, and then he and Nelson had a long argument about whether Garry Kasparov could ever have beaten Bobby Fischer at chess.

By the time I staggered through the door, I was exhausted. When I got upstairs, I saw a light on in my parents' room. Dad must be in the Black Hole, working on his article.

But when I reached the bedroom, I didn't hear the clattering of the old Remington. Instead, the closet door was shut. Against the far wall of the bedroom stood a brand-new desk, where my father sat staring intently at the glowing screen of—a computer.

"Dad! Where did you get that?"

The muted clicking of the keyboard stopped, and my father turned around. "Mattie! I didn't hear you come in. Hey, take a look at what Lyle Davis brought over." He beamed proudly.

"Cam's dad?"

"He thought it would help your mother track the election results tomorrow. But then I got to thinking—this is just what I need to get my article done."

He began to describe the features of the new computer. I listened in silence. In the space of five hours Dad had gone from being General Patton in the Black Hole to the command module of the Starship *Enterprise*. It was pretty impressive.

"Gee, can I use it for my homework sometimes?"

Dad's brow furrowed. "Well, I'll have to give you a few lessons on it first."

"Oh, come on. Pru and I already know how to use computers. They have them at school." I leaned closer and peered at the screen. But, instead of my father's article, the screen was filled with a colorful array of instruments and dials.

"Just some interactive software Lyle's working on," Dad said. "For a jet fighter simulator. He thought with my background as a military historian, I could help him work out some of the kinks."

"Oh," I said.

"It's kind of a research consultant position," he added. "Technical support."

"Sure, Dad." I understood, all right. Instead of Frank Sinatra records, my dad was now hooked on video games.

I left him consulting, and went down the hall to my room. Winston was lying on the bed, and I picked him up and rolled him into a little ball against my stomach, where he purred contentedly. Tomorrow I'd have to tell Cam I couldn't take him to the dance. And I wasn't looking forward to it.

A little while later, I heard footsteps on the stairs. They continued down the hall to Pru's room. I waited a few moments. Then I went down the hall and tapped at the door.

"Hi," I said. Pru was hanging up her jacket. When she turned around, her face was flushed and happy.

"Wasn't that great, Mattie? Our first benefit! I thought it was a real triumph. Didn't you?"

"Definitely," I said. "Sort of a Minerv-Aid concert. But how did you get Arthur to do it? I thought he was completely apolitical."

Pru shrugged. "I told him we'd kick him out of the band unless he showed up. Anyway, did I tell you? Mom says I can get a guitar. As long as it's not electric, and I take lessons. And I practice quietly."

First Dad, now Pru. I felt like Dorothy in *The Wizard of Oz,* watching hearts and brains and courage being handed out. But not even a hundred ruby slippers could solve my problem.

"That's wonderful, Pru," I said. Then I sank down on the bed and sighed.

"What's the matter?" she asked. "You look terrible. Did something happen?" She came over and plopped down beside me.

"Sort of," I admitted. And then I told her about asking Cam and Nelson to the dance.

"So now what do I do? Cam will probably never speak to me again, and I don't really blame him. And Nelson thinks he's Eliza Doolittle going to the Royal Ball—he'll probably rent a tuxedo for the occasion!" I jammed my chin down onto my fists. "I just wanted to make everybody happy. But instead, I've only made things worse!"

Pru didn't say anything. Then, after a moment, she started to laugh.

I gave her an annoyed glance. "What's the matter with you? This isn't funny, Pru. After Friday night, my life will probably be over!"

Pru stared at me. Then she burst into another round of giggles.

"Stop it! Stop laughing like a hyena, and give me some advice!"

Pru hiccupped. Then she looked smug. "But Mattie, it's so simple," she said finally, before the giggles grabbed her again.

"What is?" I was starting to get mad. The one time I confided in Pru, she acted like a total lunatic. "What are you talking about?"

"The solution to your problem. It's so obvious, Mattie. Just go to the dance with *both* of them."

I glared at Pru. "But I can't go with both of them. It would hurt Nelson's feelings. And I don't think Cam would be too thrilled either."

"I don't mean you, Mattie," Pru said. "I mean, both of you." Pru reached over and picked up one of the Paramedics purple sweatshirts. She tossed it into my lap.

I looked at Pru in her purple sweatshirt. Then I looked down at my lap.

"Oh," I said, as the obvious solution began to dawn on me. "I'm starting to see what you mean. *Both* of me." And then, hugging the sweatshirt, I started to laugh too.

fourteen

~~~~~~~~~~~~~~~~~~~~~~~~~~~~~~~

At ten o'clock, we all gathered to watch the news. The story on Minerva seemed awfully short to me, but Mom was excited.

"Thirty seconds is a big chunk of airtime," she explained. "Besides, it was the second story after the lead-in. That means a lot of people saw it."

"But they left out the part about Nelson! All they said was that Minerva was helping the shelter negotiate a new lease. That's good, I guess, but I didn't hear Harvey's name in there anywhere."

Mom patted my hand. "I can't say that surprises me. But don't worry. I'm sure it will make some of the papers tomorrow."

Election Day dawned dark and rainy. When I got downstairs, my mother was glaring out the window at the raindrops splashing against the glass.

"It's hard enough to get people to come out to the polls in good weather." She sighed. "This means there'll be a low turnout, and that doesn't usually help the underdog."

"Are we the underdog, Mom?" I asked.

She nodded ruefully. "At this point, I'd say so, Mattie. But I'm sure the coverage of last night's rally will help."

"Can we stay up tonight and watch the returns?" I asked, grabbing a muffin hot from the oven. Win or lose, I wouldn't miss the smell of chili powder in the morning. As Pru said, even Mom's mossy muffins could grow on you after a while.

"We'll see," Mom said. "But if it gets too late, Dad and I will make sure you know the results the minute you wake up."

From the time we were little, my parents had worked out a system to let us know who won important elections. If the candidate my parents liked got in, they drew a heart on a piece of paper and taped it to our bedroom door. If our side lost, they drew an X. This time, I hoped Minerva would win us a heart.

When I got to school, I headed straight for the library. Nelson was hunched over a table, scowling at the morning papers. He made room for me and then shoved over the front section of *The Gazette*.

"It must be a conspiracy, Darwin," he muttered. "I mean, Mattie. The guy's coming out of this clean as a whistle."

I skimmed through the story about Minerva's rally. There was one paragraph on the Octopus Group and their attempt to buy up the mission property. But sure enough, Harvey's name was nowhere in sight.

"What's the matter with these people!" I groaned, as Mrs. Bargreen poked her head out of the library office to see what Nelson and I were up to. "I watched Minerva hand out copies of that proposal. All the reporters got one. So how come they didn't write about Harvey?"

"Maybe they did," Nelson said. "And then maybe somebody made a phone call, and the story got killed."

"But what's the point of having a newspaper," I sputtered, "if they don't report the *news*?"

Nelson blinked at me patiently. "Mattie, look at it this way. Most of the time, all we get is somebody's version of the news. So that means whoever the somebodies are, the stuff they tell us—or don't tell us—is hardly an accident. Take a look at this."

Nelson turned to the editorial section. There, in big black letters, were the newspaper's official endorsements of the candidates. *The Gazette* was supporting Harvey Jenkins.

I scowled at Nelson. "What do you suppose they got for printing that? A brand-new quality import?"

Nelson raised his eyebrows. "Try advertising," he said. "But it's a free country, Mattie. The paper's allowed to endorse whoever they want. You and I don't agree with them, of course, but unfortunately we're not old enough to vote. Still, I'm sure there's plenty of people who won't be swayed by what they read in the paper."

Sometimes Nelson's Vulcan logic could drive me up the wall.

The bell rang, and I picked up my books and started down the hall. To my surprise, Nelson scrambled after me.

"Er, Mattie? Are we still on for . . . for Friday?"

I stared at him. "The Sadie Hawkins dance? Well, sure, Nelson. I invited you, didn't I?"

Nelson nodded. "Just making sure you hadn't changed your mind," he said. All of his Spock-like logic had suddenly vanished. He swiped a strand of black hair out of his eyes and gave me a worried glance. "People do, you know, all the time. Change their minds, that is. It's practically a law of nature."

"Well, relax, Nelson," I told him. "I officially endorse you as my candidate for the eighth-grade dance. Okay?"

Nelson gave me a relieved smile. "Okay," he said. And then he turned around and trotted back to the library, where Mrs. Bargreen was waiting with a cart of books for him to shelve.

I hurried down the hall to my math class. Halfway there, I was intercepted by Heather.

"Did you hear the radio interview with Harvey this morning?" she demanded.

"No, and I don't want to think about it. I'm trying to remember what happens when a train leaves Chicago traveling at eighty miles an hour. We're having a time and distance quiz in Mr. Garofalo's class."

"But, Mattie, now Harvey Jenkins is taking credit for saving the shelter! He's turned the whole thing around to make it look like the new lease was all his idea."

I sighed. "The guy's a snake, Heather. But look on the bright side. If no one had blown the whistle, there wouldn't be any new lease. Right?"

I started down the hall again. Heather raced after me. "But maybe next time no one will know until it's too late!"

I tried to smile reassuringly. "Look, don't worry, Heath. Because I'm sure there won't be a next time, okay? I just know Minerva's going to pull through. It's in the stars."

But by six o'clock, even Chloe had to admit the stars could sometimes be wrong.

"Why, of course!" she suddenly exclaimed. "Mercury's in retrograde. How could I have forgotten that?"

I sat glumly in the Davises' kitchen, watching the local news anchors calmly report on the early results. "And at this hour, Jenkins is leading Hightower by a substantial margin," the woman anchor said brightly, and I stuck my tongue out at the screen.

Cam was sprawled on the floor, playing with Pepperoni. "Mercury?" he called. "What do thermometers have to do with anything, Mom?"

132

"Not the element, Cam, the planet. It influences communications. A few times a year it goes a little wacky and messes things up." Chloe sighed. "Unfortunately this just happens to be one of those times."

"Well, why can't it mess up Harvey?" I said, as Pepperoni began tugging at my shoe laces with her little puppy teeth. "Why does it have to pick on our side?"

"It tried to, last night," Cam said. "But good old Harvey must have ducked."

"Shh." Chloe held up her hand. "They're switching to campaign headquarters."

Minerva stood next to the reporter, smiling confidently into the camera. In the background, I could see Sally's red top knot, bent over a computer printout.

"Our numbers are projecting a win in your opponent's column, Mrs. Hightower," the reporter said flatly. "The voters seem to be saying they aren't ready for some of the sweeping programs you've campaigned for. Any comment?"

"Only that the polls don't close for another two hours," Minerva said, her chin held high. "And I'd like to remind your pollsters that numbers are hard to judge sometimes. Our own samples indicate that this race is going to go down to the wire. And when it does, we think the numbers will tell a different story."

The reporter faced the camera. "That's the word from the Hightower headquarters. Tough talk from the underdog in this hotly contested city council race.

And now I understand we're going to switch over to the Jenkins camp."

The quiet scene at Minerva's headquarters suddenly gave way to a hotel ballroom full of boisterous people. Harvey Jenkins, looking flushed and happy, shouted answers above the screams and whistles of his raucous supporters.

"Turn off the sound," Cam groaned. "If he starts claiming victory, I think I'll throw something at the TV."

I reached down and stroked Peppy's ears. I didn't feel like throwing anything. But there was a sad, heavy feeling in my stomach, as if I'd swallowed too many jalapeño peppers and the taste wouldn't go away.

It still hadn't gone away a few hours later, when Dad and Pru came over to join the Minerva watch. Lyle left to go pick up a super deluxe pizza, but when he came back, no one had any appetite. The polls had barely closed, but every station was naming Harvey as the winner.

"Don't forget those absentee ballots," my father said. His voice had a phony, hearty ring, as if he was trying to convince us of something he didn't really believe himself. "Sometimes they can really turn things around."

"But only in a very close race," Chloe put in, and everybody went back to staring gloomily at the awful numbers on the screen.

Pru nudged me. "Maybe Minerva's twin should have come out here and campaigned too," she whispered. "Because I have a terrible feeling there's going to be a big black X on the door when we get up tomorrow."

"I don't think we'll have to wait that long," I whispered back. Pru nodded, and then tried to pretend she didn't mind by picking all the black olives off the top of the pizza.

At nine-thirty, Minerva threw in the towel. She made a lovely concession speech, thanking everyone who had supported her and vowing to continue working for the environment and the homeless and all her other programs. I only listened to half of it, though, because at that point the sad, burning feeling in my chest suddenly got very bad, and I had to go outside and take some deep breaths of cold night air.

I don't care what anyone says—not the football coaches, or the people who write self-help books, or even my own mother. Losing is horrible. Especially when something matters a lot to you. It's ugly and scary and depressing. And it hurts.

I didn't realize how much it hurt until I heard Cam come out on the back steps and felt his hand on my shoulder. He muttered, "Come on, don't let it get to you." Except I could tell the losing part bothered him too, because his hand was trembling a little, and he let out a long shaky sigh.

"It's not fair!" I burst out. "We all worked so hard.

And besides, Minerva deserved to win! Not creepy old Harvey."

A hot tear was wiggling down my face, but I ignored it. "Minerva was really trying to help people, not just make them think they were getting something for nothing." I shook my head. "Well, so much for trying to do some good. I'm never going to try to make a difference, ever again!"

I knew I sounded like Pru, griping about the Frozen Doughnuts. Except that this wasn't just a battle of the bands. I thought about Pepperoni, and the poor guy who couldn't vote because he didn't live anywhere, and all the crummy things that Harvey Jenkins had said during the campaign just so he could get elected. The lone tear rolled all the way down to my chin and stuck there, and then another one rolled after it.

When I finally looked at Cam, he had a worried expression on his face, as if he was afraid I might hit him, or faint, or jump in the hot tub with all my clothes on.

Instead he patted me awkwardly on the back. "Come here," he said. "I want to show you something." Then he took me by the hand and led me back through the kitchen and upstairs to his father's study.

The study was crammed with every kind of computer and monitor ever built. Cam went over to a TV set in the corner and pressed a button. The next minute, the screen lit up, and I saw myself sitting at our kitchen table, a determined look on my face, stuffing envelopes.

"Sometimes politics begins at home." It was Nelson's voice on the sound track. "But it only works when everyone gets involved." The next shot showed Chloe standing on a street corner, energetically handing flyers to the people hurrying by.

"When did you guys do this?" I asked. "Where was I?"

"Shh," Cam said, and pointed at the screen.

I saw Mom pausing from a phone conference to give the camera a smile and flash the V sign; I saw Minerva bustling around her headquarters, addressing the rally, dishing out chili. There were the Paramedics, playing as if their lives depended on it. And Mrs. Yamamoto warming her hands on the coffee urn. And Nelson with his megaphone.

"Win or lose, a campaign brings people together. Very few of them are paid for their time. Working on a campaign means long hours, headaches, sometimes empty stomachs. So why do they do it? Because they want to make a difference to their community. And to themselves."

The documentary ended with a freeze-frame of Minerva, standing on the steps of the shelter with her head held high.

I turned and looked at Cam. "Great job," I said. "And I'm sure we'll get a good grade on our project.

But that doesn't change anything. Everybody worked together, but it went for nothing. The good guy finished last."

"But it didn't go for nothing, you idiot," Cam said. "I bet you didn't know anything about politics when we started this. Or anything about Seattle. I sure didn't. I didn't know how much money it costs to print flyers, or run a radio ad, or feed a roomful of volunteers. I didn't really think about the people down at that shelter, or why companies don't try to clean up pollution. And I didn't really care either."

"Like Arthur," I said.

"Sure, like Arthur. Like a whole bunch of people. Well, I'll never look at stuff that way again. And neither will you. I mean, you've changed too, Mattie."

"I have?" I gulped. "How?"

"You got worked up about stuff. You even forgot about Briggs, you got so involved in Minerva's campaign. And you've got great ideas. Look at that business with the shelter. You really went out on a limb, and it paid off. So who cares if we're stuck with Harvey for a few years? Maybe he'll watch his step from now on. And maybe the next time we work on a campaign, it'll be different."

He leaned forward and peered into my face. "Right?"

I swallowed hard. "I—I guess so."

And then Cam did something that really snapped me

out of my depression. Right there in his father's study, Cam Davis kissed me.

Well, pecked me, anyway. It was over in a split second, and then we were both dying of embarrassment. But all of a sudden the bitter, exhausted feeling in my chest was gone, and there was a big, warm feeling in its place.

And then I remembered the dance.

I looked at Cam. He gave me a shy grin. Maybe, I thought, this wasn't a very good time to tell him about my latest great idea.

In any case, he'd find out soon enough.

fifteen

~~~~~~

After we had sat through all the victory speeches, and all the pizza was gone, Pru and Dad and I headed home. When we got there, Sally was sitting at the kitchen table, scribbling out another list.

"Don't worry," she said, looking up with a tired smile. "No more campaign stuff for a while, I promise. I'm just writing down food we need to order for the Golden Goat. Someone was telling me about a good place to buy fresh spinach—"

She didn't finish, because my father went over to the table and scooped her up in a giant bear hug. Then he dug something out of his pocket. He handed it to Mom. "I've been saving this to give you," he said. "Kind of a token of my esteem."

Sally looked down at the object in her hand. "Oh, John. It's a Eugene McCarthy button. From 1968 . . . the year I went Clean for Gene."

Dad nodded proudly. "Found it when I was cleaning out the Black Hole," he said. "Reminded me of what this whole thing was all about."

She was still gazing down at the McCarthy button. "And what is that?" she asked softly.

He stroked his beard for a moment. "Hanging in there," he said finally. "Not leaving it up to other people. And I've got to hand it to you, Sally. For as long as I've known you, you've never left it up to the other guy. You've always waded in there and joined the battle." He studied her admiringly for a moment. "I have to say, you'd have made a darn good soldier."

"Except that I'm against war," Sally reminded him.

"Well, okay, *apart* from that . . ." Dad shoved his hands in his pockets. "Anyway, I guess I'm just trying to say I'm proud of you, Sal. And if you ever want to try it again, you've got my vote. Besides," he added, "I think I'm starting to get the hang of running a household." He shot me a sidelong glance. "Give or take a few rough patches."

Sally looked around at us. "Well, I'm proud of you guys too. Pru, you entertained the troops. And Mattie, you came forward to help Minerva. Not to mention stuffing a million envelopes. You were all great."

Then she smiled at my father and reached up to pin the McCarthy button to the front of his shirt.

"You know, Minerva and I were talking to Bob Kelly down at the shelter. He thought we did such a great job with the rally, he asked if we'd organize his Christmas food drive. And this time, really get the community involved. Now, I figure if we start with the supermarkets and restaurants, we can . . ."

When I left the kitchen, Mom was still outlining her plan for a citywide food bank. My father was right. She was incredible. With Mom, there was always another battle to fight, another problem to solve, another campaign to wage.

I remembered how Pru had accused me of sounding just like Mom. Maybe, I thought as I started up the stairs, that wasn't so terrible.

Except that when I had kids, I'd let them eat Frosted Flakes whenever they wanted to. And when they turned thirteen, I'd understand if they wanted to wear makeup once in a while. And panty hose. And I'd definitely teach them about how to handle fine washables.

Then again, I decided, as my mother's determined voice floated up the stairs, nobody's perfect.

The next night, Pru and I met in her room to go over our plans for the dance.

"We should at least tell Cam," I said. "I mean, he's going to figure it's both of us sooner or later."

"But by then it won't matter," Pru insisted. She had all our clothes spread out on her bed and was trying to decide what we should wear. "I mean, if we both look alike, what difference will it make which of us dances with Cam or Nelson? The point is, you invited them, so that's who they'll think we are."

I was starting to get a headache. Except for a few

times when Pru needed to "borrow" my study period and I took one of her classes, we had never deliberately tried to fool anybody. Now I was glad. Deception wasn't just dangerous, it was downright confusing.

"Look, Pru," I said, one last time. "Why not go ahead and ask Cam to the dance? I won't mind, honest."

"I can't," Pru said. She held up a dress, squinting at it in the mirror. "I'm going to the dance with Arthur."

I leaped off the bed. "*Arthur*? But you told me he was too old for a junior high dance."

"Well, considering he'll be there anyway, I went ahead and invited him." Pru turned and gave me an innocent smile. "Didn't I tell you? The Paramedics are going to play at the dance."

She turned back to the mirror. "But don't worry, Mattie. I can probably get in a few dances with Cam between sets. Or Nelson, for that matter."

"Not to mention Arthur," I said grimly.

It suddenly occurred to me that if you looked at this a certain way—Pru plus Mattie Darwin, divided by Cam Davis, Nelson Richfield, and Arthur Boyle—I now had *three* dates for the Sadie Hawkins dance.

As I watched Pru try on one outfit after another, I wondered if I might have set a new Puget Sound Academy record. One thing was clear: I was seriously going to have to start paying more attention to math. Because, as far as I was concerned, this equation could only add up to one thing: complete, total disaster.

Heather was in charge of decorations. "What's the theme of the dance going to be?" I asked, as we were waiting for the bus after school on Friday. "How about endangered species? You could hang whales and California condors all over the gym. With maybe a simulated rain forest over by the refreshment table."

"Very cute, Mattie. Actually," she admitted, "I thought about doing something on the shrinking ozone layer. But I couldn't figure out how to work it into the decor."

"That's okay," I told her. "Once all those kids are packed into that gym, I guarantee you'll have an instant greenhouse effect. Global warming on an eighth-grade scale."

The bus arrived, and we got on. Heather turned to me. "Well?" she said. "Who did you finally ask? Cam or Nelson?"

I hesitated. Finally I said, "You'll find out tonight, Heather. But I promise, you won't be disappointed."

Heather nodded, mystified.

"What about you?" I said quickly. "Did you ask anyone to the dance?"

Heather looked embarrassed. "I asked Ron. But he said he'd have to ask his mother first." She sighed. "Can you imagine that? Unfortunately, his mother said it was okay."

Heather slumped against the seat of the bus. "I guess we have the opposite problem, Mattie. You have too many choices, and I don't have any."

I felt like telling Heather that I'd trade problems with her any day. Then I pictured Ron, who was about four and a half feet tall, and had red hair that stuck up like a paintbrush, and I figured I'd stick with the problems I had.

That night, Pru and I put on our identical clothes— red sweaters and black leggings. Then we sat in front of Pru's mirror and applied a touch or two of identical makeup. Pru wanted to wear Sunset Crimson lipstick, but I convinced her that Primrose Pearl was more my color. "After all," I pointed out, "we're both supposed to be me, right? So I should get to choose."

Pru had to admit I had a point. I handed her the lipstick. After she put it on, we studied ourselves in the mirror.

"I don't know," I said finally. "Are you positive you know how to be me?"

Pru raised one eyebrow, which had grown in since her disastrous plucking experiment. "Believe me," she said, "it's easy. All I have to do is talk a little lower, and kind of twirl the ends of my hair, like this . . . Oh, and roll my eyes up at the ceiling once in a while. You do that a lot, Mattie." Pru demonstrated. "See? Instant Mattie."

"I can't believe this! You mean, I have all these

horrible habits, and you've never told me?"

Pru shrugged. "Hey, you asked if I knew how to be you."

"Well, I'll never ask you again!" And I rolled my eyes.

The plan was that Pru would go next door and pick up Cam, and then Chloe would drive them to the dance. In the meantime, Dad would take me over to Nelson's. Nelson wanted to have his mother take us, but I told him that since he was my date, I was providing the transportation.

My father nodded appreciatively as I climbed into the car. "You look very nice," he said. He sniffed. "Smell nice too."

"Is it too strong?" I asked. I had splashed on some of my mother's French cologne, which she kept in the bottom drawer of her bureau and hoarded for special occasions.

Dad paused to consider. Then he shook his head. "I don't think so, Mattie. After all, what's the point of wearing perfume if nobody can smell it?"

We drove off toward Nelson's house. When we stopped at a red light, Dad cleared his throat. "I got some good news today. The editor at *The Journal of Military History* liked my latest revision. After three and a half years, they're finally going to publish my article on the Battle of the Bulge."

"Dad, that's great!"

He smiled happily. "I think the computer really did the trick. Should have gotten myself one of those a long time ago."

"What's next?" I said. "Are you going to write an article on the Battle of Marengo?"

The light turned green, and Dad put his foot to the accelerator. "Actually," he said, "I thought maybe I'd try my hand at a book this time."

"A book!" I did a quick calculation. If one measly article had taken him almost four years to write, a book would probably take forever. "What kind of book, Dad?"

Dad was frowning at the road ahead. "Actually, Mattie, I was thinking of writing a cookbook."

Fortunately, before I could answer, we pulled up in front of Nelson's house. "Just wait here," I said. "I'll be out in a second." I paused. "And no matter what Nelson's wearing, promise you won't laugh."

Dad nodded solemnly. "Mattie, you have my word of honor."

As I approached the front door, I felt a qualm. I didn't really think Nelson had gone out and rented a tuxedo. At the same time, I wouldn't actually put it past him.

Nervously, I rang the doorbell.

Mrs. Richfield answered the door. "Why, hello, Mattie. What a pretty sweater! Come right in." She held open the door and I stepped into the front hall.

"I remember asking a boy to a ladies' choice back in high school," Mrs. Richfield said. "I only hope he was half as excited as Nelson is. Nelson!" she called. "Your date is waiting!"

"Okay, Mom. Just hang on a sec."

For an endless minute Mrs. Richfield and I stood and smiled at each other. Then, abruptly, Nelson appeared.

I tried not to stare, but it was impossible. Nelson's black hair was short and clean and combed away from his forehead. In place of his mad genius sportshirt with the pocket protector, Nelson was wearing a denim button-down under a navy blue pullover sweater. And jeans. And a pair of Adidas.

In other words, for the first time in his life, Nelson looked like . . . well, an average boy.

"Nelson, what happened?" I said before I could stop myself. "I mean—you look great!"

Nelson shoved his hands in his pockets. He took an embarrassed swipe at an invisible lock of hair. "Hey, so do you," he offered. Then he looked at his mother. "I guess we'd better be going. See you later, Mom."

Mrs. Richfield was beaming. "Have a good time, kids. And say hello to your mother for me, Mattie. Tell her if she needs an extra pair of hands for the Christmas food drive, I'm available."

"I will," I promised. Then, a little stiffly, Nelson and I walked out to the car.

"So," he whispered, "do I look appropriate?"

"Entirely," I whispered back.

"I feel like a conformist," he muttered as he opened the door to the car. "Like I've lost my identity."

I patted him on the shoulder. "Join the club," I told Nelson. And then we were on our way to the dance.

It felt strange to be walking into school at night. The same gym where Mrs. Schaefer taught gymnastics now seemed dark and mysterious. The theme of the dance turned out to be *Star Trek: The Next Generation*. Heather and her decoration committee had really outdone themselves Trekking up the gym. Colored lights swam around the floor at warp speed, while mysterious Klingon shapes lurked in the shadows.

"Looks great, doesn't it?" I smiled at Nelson as we lined up to get our hands stamped.

But he was staring past me. Just ahead of us in line, Pru and Cam were filing into the gym.

When Nelson looked back, there was a wary expression on his face. But he didn't say a word.

"Come on," I said after I'd paid our admission. "Let's go get some refreshments."

"Sure, Mattie," he said. Then he paused. "It *is* Mattie, isn't it?"

"Of course, it's Mattie. Good grief, you sound just like Mr. Briggs. And speaking of Mr. Briggs, isn't that him over there, standing with the chaperones?"

Sure enough, there was Mr. Briggs, smiling and tapping his foot to the music. I was just about to steer Nelson over toward the soft drink table, when I heard a voice boom out. "Mattie! Mattie Darwin! I'd like a word with you about that documentary project."

"Uh-oh," I told Nelson. "Time to get some punch."

But it was too late. Briggs was heading in our direction.

And then, at the last minute, he veered off, and I saw him pause in front of Pru and Cam. At the same moment, Pru suddenly spotted me. Then Cam's eyes followed.

He studied me for a long moment. When he looked back at Pru, I saw the confusion swirl over his face.

"Come on, Nelson," I said desperately. I began to tug him in the opposite direction. "I'm really dying of thirst."

But Nelson had grabbed my hand and was marching over to where Mr. Briggs stood talking to Pru and Cam.

"Hi, Mattie," Nelson announced in an even voice. "Or are you Mattie?" he added, turning back to me.

Mr. Briggs paused to take this in and then chuckled jovially. "That's just what I was telling Mattie here—the sight of you girls would be a great plus for our debating team. Throw the other side off their supporting argument completely. I really wish you would consider joining the club. You too, Pru," he said, nodding to me.

By now Cam was peering intently at me too. Pru

150

frantically began twirling her hair and rolling her eyes, but it was too late. The jig was up.

And not a moment too soon. Because before I knew what was happening, Arthur Boyle had appeared and grabbed my elbow.

"Showtime, Pru. The rest of the guys are outside. You've got to tell us where to set up the equipment."

I looked around to see five sets of eyes boring into me. I was suddenly aware of the heavy cloud of *La Nuit* hovering around my head. It smelled sickeningly sweet in the hot gym, and I could feel myself breaking into a cold sweat. For a moment I considered turning and racing out of the gym. Maybe I could have my parents enroll me in a different school, I thought— someplace where I'd never have to face any of these people again. Someplace like Chicago.

Make that a boarding school, I decided, as Pru glared first at me and then at Arthur.

And then the grim silence came to an abrupt end. I heard a loud sputtering, choking sound. Then I realized it was laughter. It was coming from Cam.

When he could finally speak, he pointed at Pru.

"Arthur," he said, "I think you have the wrong girl. This is the one you want. Mattie," he said to me, "save me the last dance. In the meantime, I'm going to take Mr. Briggs over to the AV room to take a look at that video. You have the keys, don't you, Mr. Briggs?"

In silence I watched Arthur and Pru head out to the parking lot, while Cam steered Mr. Briggs off to see the documentary. Then I turned back to Nelson. He was staring down at his new Adidas, his hands shoved in his pockets.

"Nelson, I'm sorry. It was a stupid trick," I said. All around us kids were pouring onto the gymnasium floor. A new song came on the sound system, and the room shook with the vibration of the music. "I didn't mean to end up asking both of you," I shouted above the music, "it just happened. And then Pru had this brilliant idea of . . . Well, I can't really blame it on Pru. I just thought that this way, I could make everybody happy. That maybe, for once, having a twin might come in handy."

Nelson was still studying his feet.

"But it didn't, Nelson! I—I should have just told the truth and taken the consequences. I've really and truly learned my lesson. And I'll never do it again. So can't you please forgive me?"

Someone bumped into me, and I saw Ron and Heather bobbing past us in time to the music. I turned one last time to my silent date.

"Look, Nelson," I said, "I know you like me in spite of my being a twin, just like I like you in spite of your being a nonconformist. But, well, nobody's perfect, right? So just this once, can't you forgive and forget?"

As I held my breath, Nelson raised his eyes from the gym floor. With the music pounding around us, he gave me a long, agonized stare.

"Forget it, Mattie," he said finally. "You're right, nobody's perfect. Actually . . . there's something that I forgot to tell you too." His voice had dropped so low I could hardly hear it.

"What's that, Nelson?" I yelled.

Nelson gave me one last miserable look. Then he leaned over and shouted right in my ear:

"I DON'T KNOW HOW TO DANCE!"

sixteen

After I finally convinced Nelson that no one expected him to do the fox-trot, we had a pretty good time. True, Nelson wasn't the greatest dancer I've seen in my life, but he managed to make up for lost time.

Later, as we stood in the parking lot with the other kids waiting for their parents to pick them up, we agreed that everybody probably had secrets, and that honesty was absolutely the best policy.

"I was just afraid that you and Cam would hate me if I backed out on the dance," I said, fighting a sudden urge to twirl the ends of my hair. "You know, I don't think I could ever run for office," I added. "I couldn't stand the thought of anyone not wanting to vote for me!"

Nelson nodded. "I know what you mean. I guess I was afraid you'd hate me if I didn't go. I didn't know that dancing wasn't such a big deal."

He looked embarrassed. "Now, I'm not saying I find shuffling around to loud music the most enjoyable thing I've ever done—"

"Nelson . . ." I said sternly.

"But I had fun. Thank you for inviting me, Mattie. It was my first dance, and I'll never forget it."

Then he gave me a long, intense stare. For one terrifying moment, I thought that he was going to lean over and show his appreciation. It was one thing to be pecked on the mouth by Cam; getting kissed by Nelson—in public—was something I wasn't really ready for.

Instead, he gave my hand a firm, companionable squeeze. To my surprise, I squeezed back.

But when I got home, I was still worried about a few things. Cam, for instance. Even though he'd laughed off the Night of the Two Matties, and had shown up promptly to collect his dance, which turned out to be a deafening version of "Terror in the Night," I didn't feel too thrilled with the way Pru's wonderful solution had turned out.

One of the bad sides of worrying about things is that it usually doesn't make them go away. Another is that your face tends to break out.

Which is what happened as soon as I looked in the mirror the next morning. I plastered some of Pru's zit cream on the two biggest offenders, and then went downstairs, where Sally stood in the kitchen, surrounded by an army of cardboard boxes.

"Hi," I said. "What are you doing?"

"I'm sorting bottles and cans. Glass goes in here, aluminum in there." She pointed to the can crusher that Dad had installed by the door. "Here, you can crumple some cans. All the proceeds go to the food bank."

Then she gave me a closer look. "What's the matter with your face?"

"Giant zit attack," I said gloomily.

Sally frowned. "Mattie? Have you been stuffing yourself with refined sugar again? I bet if you ate more fruit . . ."

No more Frosted Flakes, I promised myself. "Just a case of nervous exhaustion." I set to work crushing cans. "Mom," I said after a moment, "do you think I'm a terrible person?"

She paused, a soda can in each hand. "Why, no, Mattie. I think you're a very good person. Sometimes you're candid to a fault, but I guess that's better than being a hypocrite. Why, sweetie? Did something happen?"

I pulled the lever on the can crusher so hard it almost came off the wall. Then, practically gritting my teeth, I told my mom about the dance.

"I mean, all my life I've tried not to do that. Trade on being a twin, I mean. But I guess I just wanted to be all things to all boys. And I thought I could be. Except it blew up in my face."

Sally smiled gently. "Yes, it kind of looks that way," she said.

I put down the can I was holding, which was now

about the shape of a tortilla. "So I'm really no better than Harvey Jenkins, Mom. I'll do anything not to lose a vote!"

Sally came over and smoothed the hair off my forehead, carefully avoiding the blotches of cream on my face. "Mattie, you couldn't be Harvey Jenkins if you tried. You did what you did with the best intentions. And I can see how tempting it must have been. But I'm sure both boys understood you didn't mean any harm."

Then, all of a sudden, she leaned closer and sniffed.

"That's funny. I could have sworn I smelled *La Nuit* a minute ago. Just what is that stuff you used, Mattie?"

They say confession is good for the soul. I looked at Mom, and figured this was my day to make a clean slate. "I, er, borrowed a little of your perfume last night. I hope you don't mind."

Sally paused and sniffed again. "A little? It smells like you emptied it over your head!"

I thought for a minute she was going to start yelling at me, but I guess she decided that I felt bad enough because she finally smiled and said, "Look, why don't you go upstairs and wash your face with some soap and water? There's a mild astringent in the medicine cabinet that will do you a lot more good than that cement. In the meantime, I'll fix some oatmeal. Now, scoot! And don't touch that perfume again!" she called after me.

After I finished washing my face, I paused outside the bathroom. Pru was in her room, practicing her guitar. So far, she could only play one chord, but she was so thrilled about it, I didn't have the heart to complain, let alone explain that in some states, being subjected to G-7th for two and a half days is considered cruel and unusual punishment.

I listened to her strum for a minute or two. Then I went down the hall and tapped on the door.

"Mom's making oatmeal. Want some?"

She looked up from her guitar. "In a minute," she said. "Want to hear the song I just learned?"

"Sure," I said. "So long as Arthur didn't write it."

Pru made a face. "Arthur!" she said scornfully. "Who's Arthur?"

I paused. "Arthur Boyle. Cofounder of the Paramedics? Your boyfriend? Remember?"

She looked disgusted. "That toad? Not on your life!" Pru picked up her guitar and banged out an angry G-7th. "Also, Arthur is no longer a member of the Paramedics. Arthur," she explained, "has defected. Last night he told us that the Frozen Doughnuts's drummer moved to Alaska. So they offered him the job. And the disloyal creep took it!"

I raised my eyebrows. "Well, you've got to admit, it wasn't the worst career move in the world, Pru. You know what they say. That's show biz."

"Well, I don't care," Pru said. She ran her hand lovingly over the smooth rosewood of her guitar. "Everybody knows that acoustic is the wave of the future. Zee and I have decided to start our own singing group. Who needs all that crashing and bashing in the background?"

To prove her point, Pru began to play her own version of "Black Is the Color of My True Love's Hair." I had to hand it to her; considering that she only knew one chord, she did a lot with it.

"'Blaa-aa-ack is the colorrrr,'" Pru sang, and her voice wasn't half bad. I stood at the window, gazing out at the frosty morning, enjoying the soft strumming of the guitar. Just as Pru got to the part about "My troooo love's hairrr," I saw a dark curly head pop up from behind the hedge.

It was followed by a wriggling little black spot: Cam and Pepperoni, out for a walk.

"Hold that verse," I told Pru. "I'll be back in a second."

And then I dashed down the stairs, thankful that Mom had made me wash the goop off my face, and gracefully arranged myself on the front steps.

"Morning," I called, as Cam and Pepperoni came around the corner. "Nice day for walking the dog."

Cam squinted up at the porch. I wondered if he was trying to decide whether I was really Mattie this time.

"Hi," he said, and I noticed again the cute way his voice cracked in the middle of a syllable, and the way the sun shone on his curly hair, and the fact that his eyes really were almost turquoise, they were so blue.

I took a deep breath. "Cam, I'm really sorry about last night. It was a dumb idea, trying to fool you like that." I paused miserably. "I just didn't want to hurt Nelson, and I didn't know what else to do, and . . ."

Cam cupped a hand to his ear. "What?" he called.

I wet my lips. "I said—"

He laughed. Then he scooped Peppy and carried her up the steps. "Heard you the first time," he said. "And it's okay, Mattie. You were just trying to be fair to everybody, and you got carried away. Besides, you guys didn't fool me for a second!"

"We didn't?"

Cam grinned. "Nope," he said. "I could pick you out of a crowd any day. You're unmistakable. And hey, you sure *smelled* unmistakable." And he wrinkled his nose.

"Oh," I said, wiping my palms on the knees of my pants. "So, did Mr. Briggs like the documentary?"

Cam laughed. "Like it? He went nuts over it. Said he was going to show it at assembly. He'll probably nominate it for an eighth-grade Oscar." He set Peppy down on the porch, and she immediately scampered over to where I was sitting. I scooped her up and settled her in my lap.

"There's only one problem," Cam added.

"What's that?" I asked, while Peppy was busy licking the skin off my face.

Cam pretended to sigh. Then he said, "Briggs thought it was so great he wants me to videotape his debating team. Said it would really improve their preparation for the state meet. Man, that guy doesn't know the meaning of the word 'no.'"

"Oh, Cam! Does that mean you'll have to go to every practice?"

Cam scratched his head. "Probably. But I told him I'd only do it on one condition. Luckily, he agreed."

I set Pepperoni on the porch, and she tumbled down the steps toward Cam. He reached down and caught her with one hand.

"What's that?" I asked. "The condition, I mean."

"Said I'd need an assistant to help me set up the equipment. Told him I thought you were the perfect candidate for the job." He shrugged. "So, it looks like you're elected, Mattie. That is, if you want to give up three afternoons a week to videotape the debating team in action."

I got up and walked down the steps. "You'll have to show me how to work all the equipment," I told him.

"Hey, it's a piece of cake. Who knows? Next stop, Hollywood, maybe. Besides," he added, with a glint in his eye, "if you can't make it, you can always send your back-up."

"Very funny," I said, but I could tell he'd meant it as a joke.

I looked at Pepperoni, and remembered the night

we'd first seen her, shivering in a cardboard box. I thought about all the envelopes I'd stuffed for Minerva's campaign, and the rally at the shelter, and the way I'd felt when Minerva lost.

And then I remembered the afternoon I'd sat in the kitchen, trying to think up an idea for my essay on "What You Can Do to Make a Difference." Maybe this was the way it worked, I thought, as I ruffled Peppy's silky ears. Making a difference, I mean. You just took things one puppy at a time. Or one envelope. Or one person.

Maybe instead of trying to save a whole rain forest, you just started with one tree.

I looked at Cam, and thought about telling him all that. But before I could, my stomach gave a loud, hollow rumble.

I blushed, but Cam thought it was funny. "Breakfast," I said quickly. "My mom's making oatmeal. Want to come in for a minute?"

He consulted Pepperoni. "What do you think, girl? Think you could eat some oatmeal?"

Upstairs, I could hear Pru starting on the twenty-seventh verse of "Black Is the Color." I had a feeling that pretty soon I'd know every word by heart. But I didn't mind.

In fact, right at the moment, I didn't mind anything.

"Sure," Cam said. "I guess I could eat a little something." He followed me up the steps to the house. "My mom slept late, so Dad made breakfast this morning. He has this recipe he thinks is really great—green tomatoes and tripe. Said he used to cook it back in college. You can't believe how gross that stuff is!"

I paused at the door and looked back at Cam.

"Just between us," I said, "I think I can."

About the Author

Mary E. Ryan was born in Manchester, New Hampshire, two minutes after her identical twin sister, Margaret. She and her sister grew up together in Tempe, Arizona, but attended different colleges and have pursued separate career paths.

Mary E. Ryan is the author of two young adult novels, *Dance a Step Closer* and *I'd Rather Be Dancing*, and her short fiction has appeared in many magazines. She holds a degree in filmmaking from New York University and the master's degree in writing from the University of Washington in Seattle, where she lives.

Although her sister, who has degrees in communications and journalism, lives in West Palm Beach, Florida, the twins stay in touch, not necessarily through ESP.

Me, My Sister, and I is a companion novel to *My Sister Is Driving Me Crazy*, which is also about the Darwin twins.

J
FIC
RYAN

Ryan, Mary E.

Me, my sister, and
I.

517338

J
FIC
RYAN

Ryan, Mary E.

Me, my sister,
and I.

517338

DATE	BORROWER'S NAME	